MW00884094

A New Dawn in Deer Isle

By

Tom Winton

ISBN-13: 978-1523803477

ISBN-10: 1523803479

Copyright © 2016 by Tom Winton
All rights reserved.

www.TomWintonAuthor.com

A New Dawn in Deer Isle is a fictional work. All the
names, characters, events and locations are from the
author's imagination or are used fictitiously. Any
resemblance to current events or locations or living
persons, is entirely coincidental.

No part of this publication can be reproduced or
transmitted in any form or by any means, electronic or
mechanical, without permission in writing from Tom
Winton.

ALSO BY TOM WINTON

Beyond Nostalgia
The Last American Martyr
Four Days with Hemingway's Ghost
Within a Man's Heart
A Second Chance in Paradise
Forever Three

Chapter 1

For thirty-five months my life had been a living hell. Every morning, noon, and night relentless flames ravaged my mind, my spirit, and my soul. You see, in 2011 my wife and I moved to that blazing-hot inferno they call Florida. And by the time we'd made it just halfway through the first nine-month summer in that overdeveloped, sub-tropical jungle, we absolutely hated the place. Then in September of the same year, with our hearts broken because we had made the move and couldn't afford to go back to Long Island, my Lorna began to weaken.

It had come on suddenly, and I told her to see a doctor. But Lorna insisted it was only because she was a little tired. She was wrong. And she'd only been feeling that way for three days when, on the way home from shopping at Wal-Mart late one morning, she suddenly felt a vice-like pressure and tremendous pain in her left shoulder and arm. Groceries in the back of the van or no groceries I rushed her straight to Martin Memorial Hospital. But by the time we pulled up to the emergency entrance, Lorna's breathing was labored. Three days later the woman I'd loved for more than forty years was gone.

I'm afraid I can't tell you where I am as I write this story because that would give away the ending and it's far too good a story to let that happen. I can't tell you if I'm in heaven, hell or anywhere in between. I may still be alive in Podunk, Alaska or living in a chalet atop the world's most scenic mountain. My mind could still be knotted in the same dark state of irreversible sadness it was three years ago, or it could have finally found its way to that most joyous of all destinations they call "nirvana." No, I can't give away any of that right now. But what I can do is start at the very beginning of my amazing journey. And if you want to come along you'd better buckle up. It's going to be one heck of a ride.

By the time Lorna had been gone two years, I'd had it with my aimless life. Ever since her death, not giving a damn about anything anymore, I'd lived the life of a miserable recluse. Day after day I woke up in my aging aluminum prison, dreading to get out of bed. I no longer bothered with any of the other senior citizens in the retirement trailer park where I lived. I didn't attend any more of their potluck dinners, go to the bingo games at the clubhouse, or take part in their community garage sales. It had nothing to do with most of the other residents at The Pink Hibiscus Mobile Home Park being considerably older than I was. That hadn't bothered me before. And it didn't have anything to do with the way the Schatz's who lived in the trailer behind mine sometimes aggravated me. Irv and Frieda Schatz were both nice enough octogenarians, but twice a week they would have a whole mob of other oldsters over for drinks and there'd be a lot of hooting and hollering going on. Sitting in their back porch every time, all of them lubed up pretty well with cocktails, they'd raise hell out there till about 10 PM. Since I went to bed at eight every night and my bedroom in the back of my trailer was only about ten feet from their porch, whenever they partied I had to pull a pillow over my head and toss and turn a while before drifting off. No, the Schatz's were okay people and so were most of the residents that went to the park's events. It was just that I wanted to be left alone.

I was no longer interested in anything. All I did to pass time was read for much of the day and watch

Jeopardy reruns on TV at night. The only time I left the trailer was when I absolutely had to. I did continue to exercise at the local gym three times a week and go to the library every Monday, but that was about it. I even cut back on my trips to the supermarket by buying enough food for two weeks rather than one. It may seem funny now that I took early afternoon naps only to break the monotony but it wasn't at the time. Neither was the slight squeezing feeling I had started feeling inside my chest. And that was happening more and more often as time went on. The whole ordeal was a soul-crushing, spirit-sucking experience. Finally, after two years of incarcerating myself, I decided to do something about it.

No matter how much anybody objected, I made up my mind I was finally going to take a trip I'd been putting off for far too long. With the way my heart had been acting up, and after what the doctor down at the VA hospital had told me, most people would have thought I was crazy to embark on such a long journey. But it was *my* life. And I was going to burn up whatever was left of it any way I damn well pleased.

The minute I got home the day of my physical examination I dialed my son's number.

"Hey, Adam, it's Dad." I said after he picked up. "How're you doing?"

"Oh fine, fine," he came back as if preoccupied, "I'm just getting ready to go to the dentist with Jessica. She's got a tooth bothering her. What's up?"

"Well tell her, her favorite father-in-law is pulling for her."

"Cute, Dad—like she has ten fathers-in-law. What's going on? I've got to get moving here."

"Well . . . I just wanted to let you know, I'm finally going to take that trip I've been talking about."

"Oh hell, you're not going to start with that again are you? Are you crazy? You know you've been getting that pressure in your chest. You can't be running all over the country. That's absolutely insane!"

Preparing to tell a little white lie, squirming in my seat, I came back with, "Not to worry, Son. I just came back from my yearly physical and the doctor said it's nothing to worry about. He said when a guy's getting up in his years it's not unusual to get feelings like that now and then. Believe me, everything is up to snuff," I lied again.

Adam didn't say anything for a moment, and it made me plenty uncomfortable. Finally, after letting out a long breath on the other end, he said, "Dad, please don't BS me. I don't believe for a second there's a doctor on this entire planet who would tell you that squeezing feeling is nothing. Now, what did he really say?"

Then it happened again. My heart flipped twice in a row, and I felt a slight squeeze both times. Quickly writing them off in my mind, telling myself it only happened because I was getting stressed, I told Adam, "Okay, he did say something about running a test or two. But I told him that if it really started to bother me I'd come back and get them."

"Yeah, there you go. You need to call him back right now and forget this *trip* madness."

"Okay Adam. Here's the real deal. The bottom line is I'm not all that worried about what might happen to me. When your mother was alive we had dreamed for years about making a trip out west and back. And she didn't live long enough to do it. I'm at the point now where frankly I don't much care a whole hell of a lot about this life business anymore. I don't like what I've seen happen to this country, your mother has been taken from me, and I just plain don't give a damn anymore."

"What do you mean you don't . . . ?"

"Please, let me finish, Son," I interrupted while straightening way high up in my recliner. "I absolutely *hate* where I live, too. I *hate* the fact that since your mother was two years shy of being old enough to be covered by Medicare the damn hospital took almost every dollar we had left from the sale of our place up on Long Island."

"That's all water under the bridge, Dad," Adam snapped back in a louder voice. "The thing now is . . . ."

"Whoa! Whoa!" I interrupted a second time. "Hold on a minute here. Just let me finish what I've got to say, okay?"

"Yeah, yeah, go ahead. I'm listening," he said in a disgusted tone as if talking to an utter imbecile.

"Good! Just calm down and listen. When your mother and I came here to Florida, all we had to live on was our social security. There was no way we could pay for health insurance. After we'd been here just short of a year, she had the heart attack. Well, guess what, I think she was so brokenhearted it killed her. Yes, granted, she obviously had a few health issues, but I *know* this place finished her off. She absolutely hated it, just as I do, and I've been stuck here three full years now. Listen to me son . . . a person can only handle just so much unhappiness and for just so long. After a while something has to give. Like I just said, that was a good part of your mother's problem and I know it's a big part of mine. I *am* going on this trip come hell or high water. Now that's the end of it. Amen."

Trying to calm myself down, I looked up at the trailer's low ceiling and let out a sigh. After that Adam finally relented. In a resigned tone he said, "There's just no talking to you Dad. Okay, go ahead, do what you want. I suppose the next thing you're going to tell me is that you're taking that beat up old van—that *green hornet!*"

"Funny, Son! Real funny! First of all, it isn't green, it's turquoise. Well, it's sort of a turquoise blue anyway. And yes, I am taking it. I just got back from getting new tires."

I wasn't about to tell him that, as always, I'd skimped and only bought two for the front wheels.

At that point I could hear Adam's wife, Jessica, talking in the background. She was telling him they were going to be late for her appointment.

"Okay, buddy, I guess you have to run," I said.

"Yeah, we're going to be late if we don't leave now. But let me ask you, when are you leaving on this cockamamie adventure? I've got this bad, bad feeling I'm never going to see you after you go. Not only do you have something wrong with your heart, but it's downright dangerous out there on the road. Sixty-six years old and you're going to drive all over the country alone? I just can't believe it."

In a voice as reassuring as I could possibly muster, I said, "Don't worry about any of that, Adam. I promise, you'll be seeing plenty more of me when I get back."

That's what I said alright. But as those last words left my mouth each and every one of them sounded tinny, hollow, and they lingered in my ears.

The plan was to leave the following Saturday morning. And for my remaining four days in Florida, I was really busy getting everything ready. The first order of business was to pull the back seat out of the van. After standing it on its side in my jam-packed little storage shed, I shot right over to Home Depot and picked up a couple of sheets of plywood, a half-dozen 2x4s, and a 5000 BTU window-type air conditioner.

Since my '99 Ford Econoline van was considerably larger than a minivan, I figured that with the rear seat out there'd be more than enough room back there. Using the wood I'd bought, I built a raised platform two feet high. And although it stretched all the way from the back doors to the backs of the front seats, I knew I'd be able to sit straight up and still have plenty of overhead clearance, even with my full-size mattress lying on top of the plywood. Not only that, but beneath the platform there would be all kinds of storage space.

Once it was all built and in place, I took out the driver's side rear window and mounted the A/C unit. Now, that job took some thought and effort. It also entailed far too much swearing as I struggled in the heat and humidity to get it just right. But I finally did. After installing the support brackets it was good to go. My Coleman camping stove easily fit beneath the platform as did a can of fuel and some boxes with dishes, silverware. I also slid under there some clothes, books, three extension cords, two fishing rods, a tackle box, and everything else I thought I might need. Already next to the mattress lay the wooden baseball bat I'd always kept at my bedside for protection—just in case I had no choice but to do a little Louisville slugging. There was no need to worry about putting curtains over the side windows or the remaining one in the back of the van. Lorna had made them with her sewing machine before she'd gotten ill, and I'd installed them a few months before she passed on. But don't think my heart didn't hurt each time I looked at them while working back there. Thinking back about how we'd planned to take this trip together brought tears to my eyes more than once.

Figuring they could easily be pulled out every time I camped somewhere, I stacked my two green plastic Adirondack chairs atop the mattress. At the head of the bed, I also put one of those tiny refrigerators like the ones college kids use in dorm rooms and stood a five-gallon bucket next to it. The bucket was going to be my washing machine during the trip. You see, I'd stolen the idea from John Steinbeck. In his great little book *Travels with Charley,* about the trek he, too, had made cross-country in his later years, he'd mentioned how he put his dirty laundry in a similar container, added water and detergent, and simply by driving, agitated the whole works enough so that when he reached a destination the clothes would be ready to hang for drying. I certainly didn't like the idea of actually paying for a new clean bucket or handing over another three bucks for the damn plastic lid but I did. I knew that even though it was a rip-off, in the long run it would beat the heck out of paying to do my laundry in coin-operated washing machines.

With everything set up in place and ready to go the morning before I was to begin my trip, I crawled beneath the van and changed the oil. And that evening Adam, Jessica and my sweetie-pie fourteen-year-old granddaughter, Dakota, came over to say goodbye. Talk about feeling blue! As soon as they left I put my gloomy self to bed. On the upside, though, the Schatz's weren't having one of their shindigs that night. And with the clock on the nightstand alongside me set for 4 AM, I only laid there for about fifteen minutes before falling into a deep sleep. Let me correct that. I should say that I fell asleep after fifteen minutes *and* another four missed heartbeats.

Chapter 2

I had never been diagnosed as having an obsessive compulsive disorder but always had at least a touch of it. I'd always been overcautious about things and have one of those minds that rarely stops racing. So, on the morning I was leaving, true to my usual form, two hours before the sun was scheduled to show its face, everything was already packed inside the van including myself. Once inside however, I forced myself to climb back out and double check the door on my mobile home. I knew I'd locked it but with my mind zig zagging in even more directions than usual, I just *had* to take a second look. But that was all the second-looking I'd be doing for a while. After pulling out of The Pink Hibiscus onto Federal Highway, I didn't bother to take a look back. And minutes later, after pulling onto nearly-deserted I-95 North in the early morning darkness, I didn't even glance in the rearview mirror. Freedom finally! For the first time in a long, long time I was actually excited about what might lie ahead. I goosed the gas pedal, got her up to seventy-five, clicked on the cruise control button, turned on the high beams and leaned back in my seat. At last, I had a future.

It was a marvelous feeling. I felt like a doomed man escaping from both a dungeon and the hangman's noose—like a high school kid waking up on the first day of summer vacation. I had no idea where I might stop later that afternoon or early evening and didn't give a hoot. I was alive again. After lowering my window I took a sip of the coffee I'd brought along and lit up one of the cigarettes I'd rolled the day before. The air rumbling in through the window was warm and humid, but since it was still dark out, I was cool enough not to have to turn on the A/C.

I hadn't been driving too long before I could feel nature calling. I had to go bad. Fortunately, I soon passed a sign saying it was only one mile to a Fort Pierce rest stop. When I got there the parking area was lit up okay by towering overhead lights, but when I got out of the van it still seemed eerie. There wasn't a restaurant or any gas pumps there. It was one of those stops that only had restrooms, vending machines, and a few half-empty racks of booklets containing discount offers for motels. What gave me an unnerving feeling was that, other than my van, there was only one other vehicle parked in the spacious lot. It was a car, and as I quick-stepped alongside it I saw it was a real beater with nobody inside. An old black Mercedes, it had fancy schmancy wheels and those impossibly-skinny tires. I knew well and good it belonged to somebody much younger than me. I did not feel comfortable going into the place but couldn't very well turn around and leave. I had to use a bathroom that badly. When you hit my age that kind of urge comes on fast, and there's no arguing with it or putting it off.

As I double-timed it toward the building, it entered my mind that I might be overreacting. But still my eyes constantly clicked this way and that. I glanced behind the bushes lining both sides of the front entrance as I came up to them, and as I hustled by them started turning my head from side to side—alternating looks back over both my shoulders.

In all reality there were two buildings beneath one roof with a wide walkthrough separating the lady's and men's rooms. And open as the breezeway was, I could see quite a bit of the back parking lot. Way back in there, parked alongside a fence in the darkness, there was a lone eighteen-wheeler. But that was it. The truck was no consolation. Odds were the driver was in a deep, road-weary sleep. As for me, I was only hoping that the driver of the Benz would come out of the restroom before I got there. But that didn't happen. The restroom door didn't budge. The only thing that did was a small lizard—a five-lined skink that scurried by so close to my toes that I had to do a quick little shuffle not to step on it. Other than the sound of my feet echoing as I did my little dance, and the high-pitched chirping of a lonely cricket somewhere nearby, everything was dead quiet. Then, when I reached to the restroom door and leaned on it, I heard something else. I thought it was one of those electric hand dryers kicking on inside, but I was mistaken —two dryers were going. After pushing the door open all the way, I saw two thirtyish men wringing their hands in front of wall-mounted dryers.

I can't tell you how much I didn't want to be in there. Believe me, neither of these characters were the kind of guy you'd want your daughter to bring home to dinner. Bad as that would be, you'd want even less to be alone with them in a deserted Florida rest stop before 5 AM. But I had no choice. I was there. And the instant I opened that door, the two of them rolled their eyes toward me—in a sinister calculating way. And what eyes they were. There were more red lines in them than you'd ever see on any road map. Both guys looked as if they'd just stepped off an all-night flight from Timbuktu but I knew better. Stoned to the gills, they had about as much right to be driving to wherever the hell they were heading as I did being trapped in this bathroom with them. Both were on the tall side, like me. One was skinny as a weed with shoulder-length, greasy black hair. The other was burly. The entire top of his shaved head was tattooed with blue and red ink. Wearing a tank top with a paunch protruding beneath it, he was built like a bodybuilder who had lain off the weights for far too long. But still he was more muscular than me. And I knew that if push came to shove, even had he been alone, he would present a problem.

If it had been the middle of the day, I would have said nothing as I walked past him toward a urinal. But it was dark as pitch. This was a sticky situation. Most everybody in their right mind was still at home, fast asleep. It felt as if there had been an apocalypse and we were the only three human beings left on the planet.

But what could I do? I had no choice but to nod at them as I walked by.

"How ya doin', *amigo*?" the skinny one said in a far-from-friendly tone that sounded more like a challenge than a question.

"I'm doing fine." I came back, looking down at the urinal in front of me, opening my zipper just in a nick of time. But don't think I wasn't fine-tuning my peripheral vision. I still had both my newfound friends in the corner of my eye.

Nothing more was said after that. And as soon as the second hand dryer stopped blowing they both walked out. I was relieved but by no means totally at ease. I knew I wasn't out of the woods yet and had a bad feeling they might be right outside that door, planning a strategy. They could still come busting back in, or be out there waiting for me.

As I quickly washed my own hands, I could hear my son, Adam's, warning replaying inside my head, "It's downright dangerous out there on the road, Dad."

After an abbreviated session at the hand dryer, I hurried back outside. Once there, my eyes again darted from side to side as I scoped out the area. I could not believe my good fortune. There was nobody in sight.

18

And the only vehicle left in the front parking lot was my van.

Feeling as if I'd just escaped imminent danger I scurried to the van, swung the door open, jumped in and cranked her up. Then I pulled back onto the dark highway and started cross-examining myself.

Maybe Adam was right. Maybe I am crazy doing this. Here I am thinking I'm going to spend two, three, four months on the road. Who knows how many more close calls I might have? Maybe I should turn around and go back to the damn trailer. No. No way. I'd rather duke it out with a back alley thug every day than go back to that hot, miserable, lonely life. The plan was to try to find a place where I'd be happier. Anyplace! No matter what happens I am not going back to that . . . to that life sentence. All I've been doing is existing. I'd rather check out right here and now than go through another day of that.

I kept going back and forth like that. One minute I was doing the wrong thing, the next I wouldn't have it any other way. But by the time I passed an exit in Vero Beach, and I could make out the first hint of rosy light on the eastern horizon, I *knew* I was doing the right thing.

It's strange how our problems, worries and fears have a way of intensifying during the nighttime hours—how we sometimes wake up in the darkness, often at some ungodly hour, tossing, turning, struggling with troubles we're sure will never be worked out. But then, after we finally drift off to sleep again and later wake to a new morning's sun, we wonder why on God's earth we had been so upset. That's exactly how I felt as I continued driving north in the first light of what they call "a false dawn." Yes, I was quickly beginning to feel more upbeat. But like I said earlier my mind is a busy cluttered place, and as all the negative thoughts lifted from it like a dense haunting fog, it didn't take long for something else to fill the new void. With the pink glow off to the right of the road ever so slowly brightening, my thoughts floated right back to Lorna.

I wished so badly that instead of the roadmap on the seat next to me she was sitting there. I reminisced about all the nights we'd talked about how great it would be to take a trip like the one I was now on. Together we imagined waking up in picturesque rural campgrounds with absolutely nothing on our minds other than what the new day might hold and where we would head to next. We'd hoped to buy a used RV—a Class A or a Class C—the kind that you drive and come equipped with a little living room; kitchen, bathroom, and a bedroom in back. I thought about the many nights we sat at the kitchen table crunching numbers. Could we afford to drive cross-country in a vehicle that only got eight or nine miles per gallon of gas? Would we be able to swing all the campground fees we'd need to pay during an eight-thousand-mile trip? What if the RV broke down? Could it be repaired by an auto mechanic or would we have to pay even more to have an RV dealership fix it? Yes, on my mind's screen I could still me and Lorna sitting in our matching recliners going over all those details. Those details and one other thing that was not pleasant.

I thought back to the times we had ended up doubting we'd ever be able to make such a trip. All too well I remembered the empty, hopeless feeling we both went to bed with many of those nights. And at that point tears welled up in my eyes and the road in front of me became hazy.

God, I thought, *I am so, so sorry you're not here with me, honey. I love you so much and always will. If I could do anything to bring you back, I mean anything, I'd. . . .*

Suddenly, as if my brain short-circuited, my lamentation ended there. I saw something, something through the windshield that derailed my train of thought right where it was. In the dim predawn light, maybe a hundred yards up the road, I spotted a slight movement. Still rolling along in the inside lane, I jutted my nose over the steering wheel and slowed the van down a bit. Just ahead, standing on the grassy road shoulder to my right there was a deer—a buck—the most magnificent specimen I'd ever seen. I don't know if its antlers had eight points, ten, or twelve. Counting them was the last thing on my mind. I was overwhelmed by this creature's beauty. And for some reason I got the strangest feeling that I was about to embark on a spiritual encounter of some kind. It was a very odd feeling, one I had never felt like that before. Then things got even weirder.

Slowing the van down even more as I approached the buck in the dusky grayness, the very first ray of the new day's sun rose on the horizon. It lit him up as if a spotlight had zeroed in on him. The creature took on a surreal look, as if it were made of neon—golden neon! And that wasn't all that was bizarre. The majestic animal was looking at me, straight at me, I mean right through the windshield and into my eyes. Forget what they say about a deer freezing in a vehicle's headlights. I was the one who was stunned this time. Nevertheless, I forced myself to take my eyes off this glorious apparition. I snapped my head back around toward the windshield and took a quick look at the road in front of me. Then I spun my head back to the right, saw that ray of light again, and my eyes followed it all the way to the horizon. It was an extremely narrow beam of sunlight—only as wide as those manmade spotlight beams we occasionally see scouring the heavens at night. It was coming from the very middle of a cloud—the *only* cloud in the sky!

Just before the van came up alongside the deer, I shot another lightning-quick glance at the road before looking out over the creature's head, beyond the distant tree line and back at that cloud again. It was a very small cloud, and it looked peculiar the way it was laying right atop of the horizon obscuring all but just a speck of the sun. But then it happened. After one more check out the windshield, I looked back and watched for a couple of more seconds. I was stunned. The bright, round magenta hole in the cloud was taking on a completely different shape. God as my judge, right before my eyes, the cloud opened a wee bit wider, and it reformed itself into the shape of a heart—a *perfect heart.*

As if that wasn't shocking enough it opened a little wider yet, and the beam of light coming through the cloud grew bigger, lighting up my face as if it was high-noon. I was absolutely stupefied. The sun's warmth on my cheeks, nose, and forehead was much warmer than was possible so early in the morning, even a Florida morning. Then the phenomenon became even more incredible. That heart in the middle of the cloud opened up wider yet. It seemed so unnatural. But the heart really did open wide enough so that the entire red sun was now smack in the middle of it—framed by it!

It was at that very moment that I felt more than just the heat on my face. I also felt the corners of my mouth begin to lift. I was smiling. It was a small smile but the most heartfelt to ever appear on my face. I knew that Lorna was sending me a message. She was telling me, "Go, George. Take this trip. Enjoy it. I love you, honey and I'll be seeing you soon enough."

Sure, I knew that most unfortunate souls who mourn the deaths of their loved ones are often desperate to find signs from them. I knew the way they sometimes hopefully interpreted things and read into them could be quite irrational. I also knew that before seeing what I just had, I'd never believed for a minute that the deceased could send signs or messages. But my outlook changed on that early morning in May. I knew then, and I still do, that what happened was far more than some kind of amazing fluke or astonishing coincidence.

As I continued up the highway I turned my head back around to take one last look at the horizon. But by now there was a tall stand of cypress trees along the side of the road. They were blocking the majestic vision I had just seen. All I could see through the succession of towering trunks were flickers of that rose-colored sunlight. But that was okay with me. In a matter of maybe ten seconds my spirits had been lifted higher than I'd previously thought they could ever again be. For the first time in three years, the world seemed like a very special place. My hopes had been resurrected. I felt like nothing could ever take them away again. And that smile on my face? Well, it stayed right where it was for a good many miles.

Chapter 3

The weather remained perfect that first morning on the road and I made good time. It was only a few minutes after twelve noon when I stopped for lunch at a Taco Bell near Marion, South Carolina. But I did not want to go inside. Still being the hermit I'd been since Lorna's death, not liking many of the changes I'd seen in our society for even longer, I didn't like eating in busy restaurants. Oh sure, once in a blue moon I would go into a mom and pop place, but that was about it.

After turning into the drive-thru lane at the Taco Bell, I told the machine beneath a giant menu that I wanted a bean burrito and a chicken taco. I also told it I wanted a cup of water, but only if I didn't have to pay for it. With that out of the way I pulled to the window, forked over the money, took a paper bag and cup from an extended hand, and drove slowly into an empty parking spot out front. I squeezed the contents of one packet of medium-hot sauce onto each of the two goodies, took a bite of the taco and picked up the road atlas alongside me.

The plan was that after reaching New York I'd take much the same route John Steinbeck and Charley did to Deer Isle, Maine when they had kicked off their cross-country journey back in 1960. After that, again as they did, I would continue to the top of Maine and double back south before heading out west. I figured I'd spend more time on the major highways than they did but still from time to time get off them and take some of the less-traveled roads and blue highways. I had dual reasons for doing that. One was to get a better taste of what America had become and you can't well do that by staying on heavily-traveled interstate highways. The second reason was that I wanted to revisit a few places

I had been to when I was much younger. I knew that seeing some of them again might foster some melancholic memories but I was ready for that. At least I thought I was.

After opening the atlas to the South Carolina map, I saw I was but a few miles from where Route 301 crossed I-95 south of Manning. Taking a sip from a straw protruding from the water cup, I recollected how I had been on 301 when I was about eight years old. Then I lifted my eyes from the map for moment. I looked at the blue sky above a Red Roof Inn Motel across the street and started doing a bit of math. I figured it must have been 1956 when I was last on that old two-lane highway. Back in those days there was no Interstate-95. It hadn't been constructed yet so U.S. 301 was the fastest route through South Carolina.

Although fifty-eight years had passed, I could still see in my mind's eye my father coming home one day in his jeans and construction boots, telling me and my brother, Oliver, to pack our clothes. He told us that early the next morning the four of us would be driving down to Fort Lauderdale for a two-week vacation. Man, was I excited. It was better than any Christmas morning imaginable, particularly since my parents rarely took us anywhere.

At that point in time we moved so often that I was already taking up space in my fourth public school in as many years. And though I had as little love for the new one as I did for all the rest, I still remembered asking my father that night, "But what about school, Dad?"

"Aw hell," he came back in his usual gruff tone, "don't worry about *school*. You'll learn stuff on this trip that you'd never learn in any classroom." And as it turned out my ill-tempered old man was right.

Still sitting in front of that Taco Bell, chewing the last of my paper-wrapped, microwaved burrito, I thought about how different things were when we'd made that trip in '56. Back then even a low-paid bricklayer like my father could afford to take his family to sit-down dinners in nice, quiet family-owned restaurants. And as if it were playing on a wide screen inside my mind, I envisioned one particular evening during the trip.

I could see my mother, father, brother, and myself inside a dimly-lit eatery—feasting on the absolute best southern-fried chicken any of us had ever eaten. Sitting at a table with a clean white linen cloth over the top and a flickering candle in the center of it made us all feel like royalty. As if the scene had just taken place a week earlier, I could clearly see the straw basket full of steaming hot, just-out-of-the-oven bread and a mound of crisp, golden chicken stacked impossibly high on a platter. There was also fresh corn on the cob and mashed potatoes drenched with scrumptious gravy. To the right of the metal tray, alongside cut-glass salt and pepper shakers were all the butter patties you could ever want. I'm talking real butter, yellow butter, and it wasn't wrapped in tinfoil either.

Yes it was all there for the taking, and delicious as everything was, the really good part came at desert time. We had slices of homemade pecan pie that were to die for. Sitting in the van, thinking back, I especially remembered the pie and not only because it was so delicious. You see, several times during the preceding afternoon, while passing so many roadside billboards that raved about the pecan products available in stores like "Stuckey's," Oliver and I asked my dad if he'd stop and buy us a pecan roll. But each time he refused even when he stopped in such a place for gas.

"Hrmph!" I now said aloud, ramming the Taco Bell paper wrappers into the bag, squeezing the whole works into a tight ball, twisting it just as tightly before hurriedly driving out of the parking lot.

It wasn't fifteen minutes after that with hopes of possibly rekindling some other old memories—happier ones—I exited I-95 where Route 301 intersected it. I wasn't on that old highway very long before noticing that sections of it had really taken their toll since the construction of I-95 so many decades earlier.

First I passed an abandoned Piggly Wiggly Supermarket. Most of the overhead letters in the store's name were missing, and beneath the few remaining ones all the windows but one were boarded up. Taped to the sole remaining plate-glass one was a warped, sun-faded *For Sale* sign. As for the parking lot in front, it only added to the place's ghostly appearance. Scattered all about were deep, wide chuckholes. For every one of them there were twice as many cracks in the time-faded asphalt. Those fissures were long and jagged—shaped like drab lifeless bolts of gray lightening. Out of all of them tall scraggly weeds had grown.

Still rubbernecking as I rolled by, I said to myself in a funereal tone, "Wow. What a dismal sight." Then I came upon an even grimmer scene.

Maybe two hundred yards up the road, also on the right side of it, I saw yet more collateral damage left behind by the construction of I-95. And just like the supermarket, the bright Carolina-Spring sunshine didn't do anything to brighten it up. There was an old strip of four storefronts, all of them deserted. As I approached the weathered building I could just barely discern the washed-out Coca-Cola advertisement that had long ago been painted on the side of the brick building. I thought for sure it had to have been done back in the 1940's or possibly even the 30's. As for the four stores themselves, like the Piggly Wiggly, there were signs in all of their windows. These seemed more desperate, saying For Sale *or Rent.* But none of them had any more hope of becoming occupied than the supermarket up the road.

A short ways beyond that building there was a shutdown truck stop. All the gas pumps alongside it had long ago been torn out from their cement islands, and the sprawling parking lot was also full of weeds and holes.

Yes, all those businesses had been in their heyday way back when I was a boy travelling up this very road. But I didn't remember them. *Eight years old,* I thought, *how could you remember?*

I was wrong. It was possible for me to recollect something on that two-lane stretch of nearly-deserted highway, but it would have to have meaning. I'd have to remember an unusual incident or event I had seen or taken part in. And that's exactly what happened next. About a quarter mile down the road, after passing nothing more than a long row of tall live oak trees, I did see something that piqued my memory. It was another building—the largest abandoned building I'd seen up to that point. And with my mind slowly spacing the words it conjured up, as if feeding my consciousness just one at a time, edging the words with melancholic and shocking emotion, I thought, *Well-I'll-be-a-son-of-a-gun!*

As I craned my neck further, straining my eyes even more to see if what I was coming up on was what I thought it was, my mind continued to speak, *That's the . . . holy cow, I think that's the very same motel we stayed at on the way south that time. What . . . what the heck is the name of this place? Does it have a pool? Yeah, I'll bet it does, right in front there behind that*

28

chain link fence that's all covered with vines. What's that sign say? It's hard to read from here. All the neon's long been broken off. Wait a minute. I can read something now. It says, Carolina Sunsets Motor Court. That's it! That's the one we stayed at. I'm positive. That's it for sure! I'm pulling in there! I've got to look around this place!

I navigated the van around a shattered beer bottle as I slowly motored toward the swimming pool. Glancing beyond it for a moment, I saw in front of the office entrance the overhang that cars used to pull beneath when checking in. Then I got closer. The overhang was sagging badly and in the center of it there was a gaping hole. The round metal posts holding it up weren't in much better shape either. Only small blotches of the original pink paint remained on the posts, the rest was all rusty. I steered around the pool figuring I'd park just outside the thing but quickly nixed that idea. There was more broken glass strewn there. Shards of broken green, brown, and clear beer bottles along with dented cans were everywhere. So were filtered cigarette butts. I assumed teenagers or homeless people must have used the ramshackle place to party.

I backed up a few feet, threw the transmission in park, killed the engine and got out. I needed to take a closer look at the swimming pool. It was where, almost sixty years earlier, I had come within one breath of drowning.

With that weed-lined fence surrounding the pool just a few steps away, I walked closer toward it. But I soon stopped dead and immediately jumped back. Wasps were everywhere. Swatting as if clearing thick smoke from my face, I hightailed it toward the middle of the pool. When I reached it I cautiously checked the vegetation on that part of the fence. With no wasps in sight I rested my elbows on top of the chain-link fence

29

and looked down. Of course there was no water in there, only more broken bottles, debris, and green moss spreading from the cracks in the bottom. I was now standing directly over the very spot where I'd almost met my demise. Right below me, plain as day, I looked down at where the bottom sloped down sharply to the deep end. The steep decline stretched across the width of the pool, and as I surveyed it a stream of dark unnerving memories quickly rushed through my head.

There was a blue-lined white safety rope right there. Every few feet there were floats on it. It ran from this side of the pool to the other—right above that drop in the bottom. Always the damn fool daredevil, I just had to push my luck that day. What in God's name could I have been thinking?

The four of us had been the only people there that late afternoon. My parents were sitting in webbed aluminum folding chairs right alongside the pool. As if I was still down there in the aqua blue water, I could see both of them in full view. My father was actually smiling about something that he or my mother had said. Oliver, my sensible brother, was on the shallow side of the rope. I, of course, just had to be on the deep side. Both of us were holding on to the rope, our scrawny bodies stretched out on the water's surface as we kicked our feet. This being only the third pool we had ever been in, and *maybe* taken to a beach as many times, neither of us could swim a stroke. But that didn't matter to me. Oh no. I got the urge to explore a little. Wondering how deep the water was I decided to stop kicking. I also let go of the safety rope and allowed myself to sink to the bottom.

Down, down, down I went until I felt that slope beneath my feet. Thinking I could simply bend my knees and push myself up, I gave it a try. Yes, I tried alright but it was a no go. The decline was as slippery as oiled glass beneath my feet, and I felt them begin to slip. As if on a fast-moving, underwater treadmill, I tried running up the thing, but my movements would only go in slow motion. *This can't be,* I thought. Then I went into a panic.

With my scrawny arms flailing and surely with my fingers spread wide open, I struggled and struggled, trying desperately to make my way to the surface. At that point the rope seemed to be ten feet away from my outstretched hands, although it couldn't have been more than one. Frightened to death, I kicked and kicked as the bubbles leaving my mouth drifted up before my eyes. I was one-hundred-percent positive that my small world was ending, but somehow I did make it to the surface.

"Help, help," I tried to holler but only gurgled instead. Tasting the chlorinated water as I swallowed it, I trained my grief-stricken eyes on Oliver for a second or two as I helplessly flailed for the rope. But he was just smiling, smiling and shaking his head—surely thinking that I wasn't going to fool him with another one of my practical jokes.

Down I went again.

With maybe a half of a breath in my lungs and the water I'd swallowed already feeling heavy in them, I started to sink. Again I did the treadmill thing, only this time I was twice as scared and panicky. I was *sure* I wouldn't make it to the top another time. But like a four-legged spider, with my limbs doing that slow motion unorthodox dance, I tried. My life depended on it. And little by little, in that silent blue underwater trap, I saw the wavy-looking azure sky getting closer.

With my neck outstretched as far as it would go, I again managed to raise my terrorized face out of the water, but this time the rope was even farther away. Seeing that while still kicking my boney legs and flapping my arms, I again jerked my sinking head toward my parents. This time they were watching me— laughing and pointing my way as if I, gasping for air and fighting to stay alive, were performing some kind of vaudeville act.

I was shocked. I couldn't believe my eyes. But I didn't dwell on their reaction very long, there was no time. I went back down, for the third time.

With even less air in my lungs than there had been the two previous times, I was sinking much faster now. I began to feel my senses dulling and my mind slowing down. I wondered if I might already be dead. Had my parents only been laughing about something else during my last glimpse of them, or had they turned into a pair of cackling devils? Were they enjoying watching me drown? Did my brother, in all reality, hate me? Had he known all along that I was really drowning? Did he not tell my parents because he did secretly hate me? Was he also a devil? Listening to my own underwater muted gags, those thoughts flooded my mind as I struggled to keep more water from flooding my lungs. Then I touched the bottom again, and I was sure those would be my last thoughts.

But the human will to survive is a strong force. With my ability to think weakening by the second, I bent my knees and tried one last time to propel myself to the surface. Knowing I'd have nothing left after this attempt I pushed for all I was worth. And as I did, despite my mind moving in slow motion, I managed one more thought. It was a question. Why on earth hadn't my parents dived in and saved me?

But when I finally reached the surface there was no time to check out their expressions or Oliver's. I was barely able to raise my nose and mouth above the surface this time. I sucked in like a heart attack victim desperately struggling to breath. No, I didn't try to look at anybody—just that rope, and as I kicked frantically my hands slowly moved closer and closer to it. At long last, I could feel it with the tips of my fingers. I kept kicking and kicking until finally I was able to grab a hold of the thing.

Odd as it may seem, I recalled all those details with fine clarity as I stood alongside the empty derelict pool, yet I couldn't bring back a single memory of what was said after I reached safety. Looking at my own shadow down there now, slowly turning my head from side to side, I realized that a bitter grimace had taken hold of my face.

I always felt like an outsider in my own damn family, I thought. *I always felt as if the three of them were sitting comfortably on a three-cushion sofa and I was constantly trying to find just a bit of space to join them. I swear, if I didn't have the old man's pale blue eyes and some of his facial features, I'd believe to this day I was adopted. Either that or my mother had had an affair, gotten pregnant, and my father always suspected I wasn't his. He sure as hell treated me like an illegitimate son. I can't remember a single conversation when he talked to me, instead of down at me. It's strange, the longer they're gone the more I resent them both. Then again maybe it isn't so strange. Sometimes it seems like the longer I'm away from people the clearer I can see them.*

I turned away from the pool and headed back toward my van. Watching my sneakered feet push aside the weeds, I walked slowly, pensively. I had forgotten about all the wasps swarming by that one section of fence but they saw me plain as day. And they didn't like it one bit. I don't know how many came at me. I started swatting and broke out into an all-out run. But I wasn't fast enough. One stung me right on the cheek.

I barked out a few words I'd rather not repeat and kept running the rest of the distance to the van. I started it up, peeled out of that parking lot pronto, and the first chance I got, sped back onto I-95 North. The hurry I was in had nothing to do with the wasps, and the sting in my cheek couldn't compare to the one in my heart.

Chapter 4

As I alluded to earlier part of my reason for taking this trip was to get better acquainted with the new version of my country and its people. For many reasons and in many ways, I felt America had devolved instead of evolved over the previous few decades. For longer than I could remember, I'd kept a close eye on things. For years I had read newspapers from front to back every day, not wanting to miss a single detail. But I didn't just *read* the printed lines, I read *between them*. I weighed every word and evaluated them. And before I stored in my mind what I read or heard on TV, I ever so carefully culled the news provider's slants, convenient omissions, and their all-too-obvious agendas. And only after all that careful perusing was done, would I allow myself to assimilate the information. Ernest Hemingway had the right idea. He often talked about the importance of having a "built-in bullshit detector" in one's mind. And I constantly tried to improve mine. My mantra had become the same as you occasionally see on a thinking person's bumper sticker—Question everything. And I did.

Nevertheless, as much as I doubted it I hoped that during my journey I would see or hear a few things that would loosen up all the negativity jarred tightly inside my mind. I may not have had long for this world, but I still had a glimmer of hope that as I travelled cross-country a little light might from time to time find its way into my apocalyptic outlook. But never did I dream that on the very first evening that would actually happen.

I had pulled into a nearly-deserted campground outside of Rocky Mount, North Carolina two hours earlier, and by that time the sun was about to set.

Savoring the cool, dry air after calling my son Adam on the office phone, I thought how back in Florida it would still be hot at that time of day. With the van backed into my assigned site, sitting in front of it sipping a beer and reading, I noticed in a movement in the brush between my site and the next one. Shifting my eyes from the pages of my book I saw it was a chipmunk. A seemingly happy little guy, he was nonetheless keeping a close eye on me as he rummaged in the grass. In the shade of the tall live oak trees surrounding the site on all sides but one, I watched the little critter go about its business for a moment or two and noticed another movement. With both my Adirondack chairs set up just a few steps from the road, I saw two people—a man and a woman, strolling my way.

Dressed in a black tank top and long jeans, the thirtyish man's head was shaved clean to the flesh. And close as they were, I could see that both his arms were covered with tattoos—from his shoulders clear down to his wrists. I also noticed a gold ring hanging beneath his nose.

Oh Geez! I thought. *Would you look at this! Why in God's name would anybody want to graffiti their body like that? And why would they stick a metal ring in their nose? Ha! I'll bet he's one heck of a deep thinker. This is just my luck. Empty as this place is, they would have to walk right by here. Oh well, I'll bite the bullet. I can't ignore them. I'll just say hello.*

The woman that the man was holding hands with was about the same age as he. But she was cute as a button and dressed quite differently. Wearing a tie-dyed tee shirt, with her sleek blonde hair hanging down past the waistline of her bellbottoms, she looked like a sixties throwback. Not only that, but with round wire-rimmed glasses perched atop her nose, she put me to mind of the bohemian intellects I'd so often seen on the streets of Manhattan during the flower-power days. The kind of girl you'd expect to find at antiwar protests or maybe eating a brown bag lunch with Alan Ginsberg on the wide front steps of the Fifth Avenue Public Library.

"Hi there!" the man said as they approached.

I rested the book on my lap, and in an equally cordial tone said, "Hi folks. How're you doing?"

"We're doing well," he said, as they both came to a halt. "Are you reading a good one there?"

Close as they were by now, I saw that he was actually a good looking young man, if it wasn't for all the decorations. But still, thinking, *sure, like you've ever even heard of what I'm reading,* I instead said, "It's *Travels with Charley,* by John Steinbeck."

"No kidding? That's a great little book! I've read it several times."

"Really?" I said in a surprised tone, "So have I."

"He's always got a book in his hands," the lady chimed in as he led her toward me and asked, "What part are you up to?"

Seeing them both in a new light now, still somewhat shocked, I answered, "The part where Steinbeck's inside a mobile home with that younger couple. I'm reading the book again to refresh my memory. You see . . . I'm on a similar trip and I plan to retrace parts of the route he and Charley took."

There was a pause in the conversation then. A big diesel pickup truck with a travel trailer in tow motored by us slowly and we all waved. Once it passed, my two visitors looked back at me and I continued what I was saying. "Yupper, Steinbeck was about sixty when he made his trip—a few years younger than I am. Nevertheless, I'm doing it."

Wrestling with my eyes so they wouldn't turn to those tattoos then, I might have been put out by what the man said next. But by the way he hiked the waist of his jeans up by their belt loops, and the polite, tactful way he phrased his words, I didn't take any offense.

"I think he was fifty-eight when he made the trip," he corrected me. "That was back in 1960."

I knew what year the Nobel Laureate author and his poodle took their trip, and I could have sworn that he was sixty at the time. Being the stickler for details I was, and like everybody else on the planet not liking to be proven wrong, I squirmed in my seat a bit when I cocked my head to the side and fired back a doubtful, "Are you *sure* about his age?"

"Oh, he's amazing when it comes to remembering such things," his perky companion cut in, "he's an English Lit professor. Or at least he *was* until recently."

"Oh stop, Carla," he said in a calm, soft-spoken way that seemed to contrast with his brutish appearance, "we all remember things that we're truly interested in." Then turning back to me he added, "Anyhow, yes, I'm sure Steinbeck was fifty-eight. He passed away eight years later, in 1968, when he was sixty-six."

To say I was impressed would be an understatement. Here was this stranger I had viewed as a freak just minutes earlier blowing to pieces my rock-solid, predetermined conception of people who went out of their way to look the way he did. I'd always thought that anybody who'd cover entire parts of their body with dark, inky drawings had to be either out of touch with reality, totally mindless, or both.

Seeing how wrong I'd been now, I laid my book on the grass beside me, rose to my feet, and extended my hand toward the man. "I'm George . . . George McLast."

"I'm Reilly Slaughter," he said, gripping my hand firmly but not overly hard like so many insecure men often do, "and this is my wife, Carla Ann."

A vivacious and friendly person, she shot her small hand right toward me. As my palm encompassed all of it, I said, "It's really nice to meet you both. What do you do Carla Ann? I mean do you work too?"

"Well, we both left our jobs, but I am a nurse. I worked in a psychiatric hospital back in Jacksonville, Florida."

"Are you a reader, too?" I asked, releasing her hand.

"I sure am. I haven't read *Travels with Charley* yet, but I've read most of Steinbeck's other books—*The Pearl, The Winter of Our Discontent, Of Mice and Men, East of Eden*, and, of course, *The Grapes of Wrath*."

I was truly enjoying talking to these nice folks. I never dreamed that I could possibly share so much common ground with people like them, but there it was, bigger than life, the first of many new lessons this old lion would learn while on his journey.

With the sun by then quickly dropping beneath the western horizon, we talked for about ten more minutes. They couldn't believe it when I told them I was eight years older than Steinbeck had been when he'd taken his trip. They insisted that I was putting them on—that I could not have been past my mid-fifties. And that, too, made me happy. I couldn't fight back the big smile spreading across my face when I told them that I'd heard that before.

Just before Reilly and Carla Ann headed back to their van, they told me where they were heading. They said that for four years they'd been saving every possible dollar so they could move up to rural Vermont. They wanted to get back in touch with nature and live off the land as much as possible. And I had no doubt they would make their dream work. For the longest time I had been telling people, and myself, that the way the world was changing, I had no desire to be young again. Yet somehow I envied the Slaughters, and I told them exactly that. They were nice, intelligent people, and they left me with a good feeling inside.

As I watched them walk away it struck me as odd, but even though there was a good chance I was approaching the end of my life, and as angry as I was at all I'd seen go downhill in my country, I got the feeling that there was a bit of hope for those I'd leave behind.

I went to bed even earlier than usual that night. And as I lay comfortably in the back of my van, I actually felt content. But it wasn't only because I'd spent a few minutes with those encouraging people. Another reason was because I realized I had only felt that unnerving squeeze in my chest a few times all day. It only happened when I was in front of that Taco Bell and motel pool, when I was thinking about my father and the rest of my family.

Chapter 5

As usual I awoke the next morning at about five. After getting dressed I went out into darkness and fired up the Coleman stove to boil water for instant coffee. Once it was made, I sat in one of the Adirondack chairs again and studied the stars I could see through the treetops. Without a single vehicle or trailer nearby, all was quiet as could be until I heard the enchanting call of an Eastern Whip-poor-will. Lowering my eyes from the sky, I shifted them toward where the sound was coming. I couldn't see the bird because it was somewhere far off in the distance, but that didn't stop me from feeling an affinity toward it. Other than the plants and trees surrounding me, it was as if the bird and I were the only living things on the planet. I lit up a cigarette and listened until I finished the smoke and my coffee. It was only the second morning in well over a thousand that I was glad to be alive. The other had been the day before, when I'd driven away from my mobile home in Florida. Sitting there now, in the North Carolina darkness, I felt as if I'd escaped from a long, maddening, spirit-crushing torture. And as I did every morning, I said, "Good morning, Lorna. I miss you hon. And I so wish you were here."

Just before the first dim glow of light appeared on the eastern horizon, I got ready to leave. I put the portable camping stove back inside its box and put it and the metal pot in the storage area beneath my bed. Being as quiet as I could, I slid one of the plastic chairs over the other, hoisted them into the back of the van, and gently closed the two back doors. With that accomplished I got in behind the wheel and slowly motored out of the campground. Still dark out, I drove up a deserted country road a couple of miles, made a left turn and saw just ahead an illuminated McDonald's sign high in the sky. That was where I'd gotten off I-95 the day before. When I reached the fast food restaurant, I steered into the empty drive through and told the speaker there, "I'd like one small senior coffee, two creams please."

"That'll be thirty-nine cents. Please pull to the second window," a young man's voice instructed me.

After doing as I was told, the still-sleepy but well-mannered teenager took my money, handed me a bag and leaned out again with the change. There was still a hint of a smile on my face when I thanked him. *Thirty-nine cents! That's more like it,* I thought while checking inside the white bag. There were two creams but no stirrer. When I told the cashier, he gave me one and apologized, but I said, "Nothing to it. Have a real good day." Then I pulled into a parking space in front and poured the contents of both of the small plastic containers, mixed the works, took a sip, put the cup into the console holder, and pulled away.

After passing a Chevron Station and Fairfield Inn, I crossed the highway overpass and hung a left onto the entrance ramp. It was a long, sweeping, curved ramp, with dense woods on the passenger's side of the van and some trees on my side as well. At any rate, when I was about halfway through the curve, I spotted a movement in my headlights. On the left just ahead, something came out from the trees, and the beams of my headlights lit up its small eyes.

As I slowed down I wondered, "What's this? Must be a raccoon or an opossum."

Slowing down even more as I approached it, I saw that it was not a wild animal. It was a dog, a little bitty one. It had stopped alongside the road, maybe two feet from it, and it was staring at the van. The poor animal looked so forlorn and so lost.

Glancing quickly into the rearview—seeing that no vehicles were coming behind me, I rolled to a full stop next to the dog and lowered the window. Leaning out of it, I said in a gentle voice, "Hey, little guy, what the heck are you doing out here at this hour?"

With its wheaten coat, and triangular ears that stood straight up, it looked like a Cairn terrier—a filthy dirty Cairn terrier. Its fur was all matted in clumps, it wasn't wearing a collar, and it had two of the unhappiest little eyes you'd ever seen. I felt so bad for it. And as if it were reading my mind, it stood up on its hind legs and leaned its front paws against my door.

"I'm so sorry little guy," I said, my head craned out the window, "I can't take you with me. I just can't."

Hearing that, as if he understood what I'd said all too well, he whimpered and his eyes begged even more. With only the sound of early morning crickets chirping in the surrounding trees, I heard his desperate message loud and clear. It was as if he was saying, "Don't leave me here! Please, don't leave me here! I don't know how much longer I can make it on my own! I don't think I'll make it through one more day of this. Please, please take me!"

The fact that he was so very thin did not make his future seem very promising. I only wondered for a brief moment how long he may have been lost or disposed of before a white light flashed across my face. It reflected from the outside mirror on my door. An eighteen-wheeler truck was rounding the curve behind me. Quickly, I pulled out the knob beneath my steering column to engage the van's flashing lights in back. And just as quickly I weakened. Yanking my head back out the window and down, with the dog now scratching the door, there simply wasn't enough time to weigh the situation in my mind. So what did I do? I went with my heart's decision and relented. "Oh hell," I said, "I can't just leave you *here*."

Shooting another quick glance out the mirror, I could see the truck was slowing down behind me. Carefully, I opened the door so as not to hurt the little guy. As I eased it open, he got back down on all fours and backed up a bit. But when I got out of the van, bent over, and extended my arms the friendly little terrier didn't hesitate. He immediately leapt into them as if I were a long lost friend.

I put him on top of the road atlas alongside me, and he instantly started panting with his mouth open in a very content way. It was as if he were smiling at me, telling me, "I really, really like you, mister." I then closed the door and threw the tranny into gear. When I pulled away I gave the trucker a thankful wave out the window. Right away he flashed his headlights lights and tapped his horn, letting me know I had done the right thing. Seconds later the dog and I merged onto the highway.

"The first thing we're going to do, my friend," I said, reaching over to pet my passenger, "is get you some water and something to eat."

Savoring my strokes across his knotted head, lowering it just a bit each time my hand ran across it, he wouldn't take his eyes off of me. Sitting there erect, still panting excitedly and looking at me as if I was the greatest thing since southern pecan pie, I had to be straight up with him. Again my words came out in the same kind, empathetic tone, but I tried to sound more authoritative. "I'm sorry my friend, but don't get any ideas. You *can't* stay with me. I can't take you."

Somehow those last words seemed to linger in the dark van—"I can't take you. I can't take you." I felt terrible, but what was I to do? Hoping my lousy feeling would soon be sucked out the open window, I tried to think the situation out.

I'll get off the highway at the next exit and head back to where I just was. I'll take him to the McDonald's I just left and get some food and water in him. Guess I'll have to stay around there for a few hours too, until the nearest animal shelter opens up. I'll turn him in and after that get back on the road. That's it. That's what I'll do. It'll set me back time-wise a bit, but what the heck I have no deadlines to meet. I don't have to be anywhere until I get there.

I then saw a sign up the road. It announced that the next exit was a mile away. I stopped petting the dog at that point, but he wouldn't have it. Obviously starving for attention, he leaped onto my lap.

"Hey! No, no, little fella. You can't stay here. You've got to get back over there."

Ever so gently I pushed his butt toward the other seat, but he whined and looked up at me with those sad eyes again.

"Oh heck! Alright! You can stay here for a minute or so, but that's it."

I meant what I said, but in just the time it took to drive that mile to the exit, a few peculiar things happened.

First off, the very top of the sun appeared above the horizon, and I instantly thought back to the previous morning. It was now almost the exact same time it had been when I'd seen that heart of sunlight break through that cloud back in Florida. "No way," I said, taking my hand off the dog, putting it back on the steering wheel along with the other. "Pull yourself together, man. This has nothing to do with that," I tried to convince myself.

But then I started to think of something else. I thought about how nice it might be to keep my new

45

friend. He seemed like a really good dog, smart, too. But I stopped myself.

No, he doesn't have a collar. And he's all bedraggled. But it is possible that somebody who truly cared for him simply lost him. He looks like he's been on his own for days, and there could be people who are worried sick. I have to take him to a shelter. The owners might have notified them that they lost their beloved pet.

But that train of thought didn't last. It crashed only a nanosecond after it entered my mind. For as soon as I lowered my hand back on the dog, I felt something. Beneath the tips of my fingers something didn't feel right. And my new friend jerked his head, and let out a painful yelp.

"What in God's name is this, fella?" I asked, shifting my eyes from the road ahead to where my fingers had separated the clumps of fur. That's when I saw it. In the new morning light, I could see there was a nasty gash in his skin. It was all raw. Glancing back and forth at it and the road, I saw that it encircled his entire neck.

"I'll be a son of a bitch!" I blurted out angrily, "You had a collar alright. You outgrew the thing. The lowlifes who owned you never bothered to take it off."

That was it. I was coming up to the exit and had just begun to slow down, but now that wasn't going to happen. I took my foot off the brake pedal and hit the accelerator. There was no way I was going back to where I'd found him. I couldn't be sure how things were going to work out, particularly since I was just beginning such a long trip, but I had good vibes about this dog. And there are times in our lives when practicality should have absolutely no bearing on the decisions we make—times when we listen to our hearts and what we hear is far louder than the distant rumblings of consequences. This was one of those times. This abused terrier was coming with me no matter what. It was a done deal.

A short time later we came upon an exit with a Burger King. I pulled into the restaurant's parking lot and told my new sidekick that I'd be right back. After gently petting his head I locked the doors behind me. Once inside, I thought it would be a good idea to go to the men's room. But first I glanced outside through one of the plate-glass windows. I'll be darned if I didn't see the top of the dog's head looking over the top of the driver's seat. He was watching me. Not wanting him to be alone out there for too long, I hustled to the bathroom, shaking my head with a smile on my face. When I came back out, I glanced out to the lot again before going to the counter. Sure enough, he was still up there.

After placing my order I took the receipt from the cashier, stepped to the far end of the counter, and leaned with my back against it. Vigilantly I kept my eyes peeled outside. I knew then that there would be times during my journey when having a dog would be difficult. Times when I'd want to go into other restaurants, stores, and the likes where pets wouldn't be allowed. But those kinds of restrictions really didn't matter. This dog was a good one, and I would deal with whatever inconveniences I had to. I'd always had a thing for lost causes, and I liked this furry one with the alert hazel eyes an awful lot. I knew I'd worry about him a lot and be overprotective at times. But that was my nature and wasn't going to prevent me from keeping him.

The Burger King was quite busy considering the early hour, but after waiting only few minutes, still keeping a close eye on my van outside, one of the workers called out my receipt number. After she handed me my bagged order, I thanked the cute little teenager with a southern accent, and I headed back outside. As I approached the van, my new road partner was looking my way through the driver's side window. He started scratching at the glass excitedly with his tail wagging to beat the band.

"Okay, okay," I said, shifting the bag to my left hand so I could dig into my pocket for my keys.

"Ruff! Ruff!" the little bugger barked for the very first time. It was as if he was impatiently saying, "C'mon! C'mon!"

After slowly opening the door only halfway so he wouldn't come out, I coaxed him back over to the passenger seat and climbed in myself. Once inside, my first order of business was to give him the water I'd gotten. As I held the cup, he lapped it up as if he'd been lost in a desert for two weeks. It caught my attention that he kept swatting at the cup with his left paw, but I had no idea at the time that most Cairns are left-pawed. At any rate, water was now splashing everywhere.

"Okay, okay. Take it easy for crying out loud. You've got to drink this, not whack it everywhere."

Of course, what I said didn't faze him until he was good and ready to settle down, but I didn't mind a little water here and there. And once he started drinking it there was no stopping him. I never would have dreamed that such a little tongue could lap up so much water so quickly. In no time at all I found myself tilting the cup so he could get his muzzle into it and finish the last of the cool liquid. It was then that I thought about the decision I'd made minutes earlier while inside the Burger Queen's bathroom. I would call him Rocky and for two reasons. Number one, I'd found him just outside the town of Rocky Mount, North Carolina. Number two, I knew that in Scotland, Cairn Terriers were used to hunt down small rodents that built their homes in the stacked rocks the Scottish used to mark graves. So, Rocky it was. And despite his ancestry, after what he'd been through, I was going to make darn sure he never worked a single day for the rest of his life or at least for what was left of mine.

Although I'd sworn off of pork and beef many years earlier I had bought Rocky a sausage biscuit. I didn't have a whole lot of options considering the early hour and where we were. But let me tell you, after he drank that water and I opened up the bag he went absolutely nutso. Once he'd gotten a whiff of what was in the bag, he started jumping around on the passenger seat like a little boy seconds away from peeing his pants. But this wasn't the time to teach him manners. Lord only knew how long it had been since he'd eaten. However, I only hand fed him bits at a time. And I did it *very* carefully so he wouldn't take my fingers off. After he finished I put the wrapper and empty cup back in the bag, mashed it up, and we hit the road again.

Chapter 6

As I merged back onto I-95 after leaving Burger King, I could tell Rocky was feeling a whole lot better. He settled down on his hind legs, put his front paws up on the dashboard, and stared ahead as if he knew were going on a great adventure.

"No, Rocky," I said, "Get back. You're going to fall in front of the seat."

Putting my right palm beneath his chest I lifted him and moved him back.

"Stay," I said, and he actually did. To my surprise he obediently lay right down and seemed perfectly satisfied to watch me drive. I, of course, didn't know what was going through his head, if anything, but I wondered if he somehow knew why I was smiling.

As we drove on he soon fell into a deep sleep. He obviously needed it and didn't wake up until I stopped for gas in Fredericksburg, Virginia.

I knew he would have to relieve himself after all the water he'd drunk earlier. So as soon as I refueled I walked him over to a grassy area alongside the Chevron station we were at. But there was no way I was going to let him out without a leash. I didn't yet have one, and we were mere yards away from all the frantic traffic zipping through the business section of town. Bumper to bumper, yet moving quickly, there were four lanes of long-distance travelers pulling in and out of town and lunch hour locals shooting around in every direction. Not knowing what to do about the leash, I went to the back of the van and rummaged around beneath the bed's wooden platform. There I found a temporary solution—my shortest extension cord. Not wanting to tie the Rube Goldberg fix anywhere near Rocky's injured neck, I carefully snugged it up behind his front legs and then led him out to a small patch of grass surrounding the base of the station's tall sign. The makeshift leash must have looked ridiculous to anybody who might have noticed it from their car, but I was concerned about the dog's safety not about appearances.

After Rocky tinkled on the grass I let him sniff around a while. And as he did my mind suddenly flooded with some more memories. Sure, before we had gotten off the highway I'd seen signs alerting me that we were approaching Fredericksburg. And I recalled that I had been there many years earlier. I even had a flashback or two, but now more fifty-year-old memories came to my mind. They were storming into it. As if the old Bell & Howell home movie projector my parents once owned started click-click-clicking inside my head, a procession of short, silent film clips started playing on that screen inside there. I can't tell you why but some of the remembrances I visualized appeared in black and white while others were in living color.

The year was 1964. I knew that because I had been a sophomore in high school at the time. It was about eight in the morning on a cold, clear January day. I'd never even heard of Fredericksburg, Virginia at the time, but I would find myself sleeping there that night. Since it was a school day I went down to the first floor of my apartment building that morning and knocked on the metal door with 1-C stamped just above the peephole. A moment later my closest pal Jimmy Brannigan came out and we headed off to school.

"Screw school," Jimmy later said out of the clear blue as we walked by the Bedford Stuyvesant Housing Projects. "Let's go to Florida, Georgie."

"Florida!" I blurted as if it the state was in another country, "Have you got rocks in your head?"

"Hell no, man! I mean it, let's go to *Florida.*" The look on his face was dead serious.

"Where the heck are we going to come up with the money to go all that way?"

"Not to worry my friend. It's in my back pocket. I've got sixty-five smackers."

And he wasn't kidding. He'd gotten the Florida idea earlier that morning and lifted the money from his mother's jewelry box after she'd gone to work. I knew that was a messed up thing to do, but when I told him he needed to take the money back to his place, he said, "No way." To make a long story short when he proceeded to tell me his idea in detail, I simply couldn't refuse. Particularly since living at home with my father had never been a cake walk. With his nasty temper, foul disposition, and all the times he'd verbally lambasted me for next to nothing, I was rarely at ease in my own home.

Jimmy's cockamamie plan was to go down to The Sunshine State and become Miami Beach golden boys. He said we could get jobs as lifeguards at upscale hotels. And once we got all tanned-up, the rich women would be all over us. That really got me thinking. Right away I envisioned myself alongside a huge swimming pool full of aquamarine water. Even though I wasn't much of a swimmer I was sitting high atop a lifeguard stand. Rushing toward me in skimpy bikinis—coming from every direction, were these gorgeous women. There were blondes, brunettes, redheads—all of them with brightly-colored drinks in their hands and propositions on the tips of their tongues. That was it! I was going!

After Jimmy and I dumped our schoolbooks in one of those big wire-mesh trash cans the City of New York put on most corners, we were on our way to a new and better life. We snuck through the turnstiles at the subway station, rode to Grand Central Station in Manhattan, and as soon as we saw a liquor store, Jimmy went in with his phony draft card and bought us each a pint of vodka. Mind you, it was still only about 9 AM.

We stuffed the individually-brown-bagged booze bottles into the pockets of our pea coats; then got two quarts of Tropicana orange at a nearby delicatessen. After that we hoofed it down crowded, rush-hour sidewalks—all the way to Penn Station on Eighth Avenue and West 31st Street. Once we got there we ducked into a men's room, emptied half of our cardboard OJ containers and poured in the vodka. Voila! Not long later we were good to go. Well, almost.

When we went to get our tickets at a booth in Penn Station there was a slight snag. The sixty dollars and change we had remaining hadn't been enough to buy the tickets to Miami. So after driving a bespectacled, bald man behind the counter crazy with questions about how far we could go for this much or that, we decided to go to Fredericksburg, Virginia. I'd never heard of the place, but Jimmy had. He had family there. So our modified plan was to hopefully spend the night with them and start hitch-hiking the rest of the way to Florida the following morning. Soon after getting our tickets, with those Tropicana containers still in hand, we boarded the train.

Considering we drank way too much, most of the trip to Virginia went fine. But things got somewhat iffy at the end of it. In our unstable condition we didn't hear the announcement when the train was approaching the Fredericksburg station. With neither of us realizing the train was coming up to it, I got up from my seat and went to the bathroom. The head was at the far end of the car, and when I came out of it three soldiers, who had obviously been smoking cigarettes between the cars, came walking toward me. They said something I no longer remember, but it definitely wasn't a friendly greeting. Looking like they, too, had been drinking, they wanted to start trouble, and there was no way I was going to take it. In no time at all I was nose to nose with one of them, and almost as quickly Jimmy appeared right beside me. Now, we might have been outnumbered and those guys were obviously a few years older than us, but we had grown up in "Bed-Stuy," Brooklyn. Between that and the fact that we were all boozed up, there was no way we were about to back down. Again, I don't recall the words that were exchanged. But seeing our fists balled at our sides and our unafraid, cocky attitudes, they all of a sudden weren't in the mood to rumble.

While all that was going on though, the train had stopped at the platform where we were supposed to have gotten off. It wasn't until the soldiers brushed by us and the train started to roll again that I noticed through a window that we were leaving the Fredericksburg station. Immediately we ran toward the middle of the car where the conductor was talking to another passenger.

"Excuse me," Jimmy said to him, "but we just missed out stop, and we gotta get off there."

Looking at us as if we were even bigger idiots than we really were, he said, "Well . . . you're just going to have to wait until we get to the next stop to get off."

"Bullshit!" Jimmy blurted angrily, "If you don't stop this train we're going between the cars and *jumping* off."

"Are you crazy?" The burly conductor said. "You're not going anywhere."

With the train picking up a little speed now, I chimed in, "Oh yeah! Well watch this! C'mon Jimmy, let's go." Then we dashed around the guy with the funny-looking hat and headed for the back of the car."

"Dammit!" he barked out, "Wait here." Then he sprinted to the front of the car, yanked a handle mounted on the side of it, and disappeared into the next car—which just happened to be the locomotive.

In no time the passenger train slowed down and came to a stop. Seconds after that it started backing up, and before you could say "Casey Jones" we were back at the station. When the doors opened Jimmy and I bolted out of there and ran down the concrete platform like two crazed gazelles—followed the entire way by the fuming conductor's shouts.

As I now looked down at the green Virginia grass around my sneakers outside that Chevron station, with Rocky in front of me still sniffing fervently, I rotated my head ever so slowly back and forth. To say the least my adolescent behavior had often been on the reckless side, and I wondered how on earth I ever managed to come out of those years without getting into any serious trouble. Standing there with the orange, electrical-cord leash in hand, still deep in thought, my mind started to shift. No longer hearing the traffic rumbling all around me, oblivious to it, another remembrance of that long ago trip found its way into my mind.

Since Jimmy's mother had grown up in Fredericksburg and still had family there, she and his father had taken him there a few times when he was younger. Because of that, but still to my amazement, after we exited that train station and jumped into a taxicab parked outside, Jimmy had actually been able to give the driver directions to his uncle's place. A short time later, as we rode in the backseat through a forest of green pines and winter-leafless broadleaf trees, Jimmy cracked me up when he told me his uncle's name was *Squirrel*. Needless to say, I busted out laughing.

"Uncle freaking Squirrel," I burst out, just before losing it completely. "Man, I gotta see *this* guy! What is he, one of the Real McCoys? Does he wear a coonskin hat?"

Rather than answering me, Jimmy leaned forward toward the front seat and extended an arm over the backrest. Pointing to the right of the road he told the driver, "Turn in there." He did, and through a maze of skeletal gray limbs and tree trunks—about two-hundred feet down a snaking, dirt driveway—I saw a small log cabin.

A moment later when we rolled to a stop in front of the place, I couldn't help myself. "Jeez, man," I blurted again, "I'll bet George Washington himself slept here, or at least Honest Abe!"

"Cute, McLast," Jimmy snapped back as he handed the cabbie a five spot, "You better behave yourself, man."

It was late in the January afternoon by this time and everything other than the smoke wafting out of the cabin's stone chimney was dead still. Well, almost everything was motionless. As the cab backed out of the driveway and we stepped to the front door of the old log structure, I did notice out of the corner of my eye another movement. Turning my head, I saw in a huge pasture behind the homestead a few thin cows slowly moseying around in the dead, brown grass. Then Jimmy knocked on the planked wooden door, and I just had to whisper to him, "I'll bet you a buck Uncle Squirrel has a musket hanging on the wall."

"Screw you," he said without turning his head, "Just behave when we go in there."

I might have been a jokester, but I did have enough sense to behave respectfully.

When Squirrel opened the door Jimmy explained to him that we were heading to Florida and thought we'd stop in to say hello. The short stout man with a protruding belly and woodsy Southern accent seemed a bit standoffish, but he did invite us in. As I followed my buddy through the low doorway, I wondered how this guy ever got the name he did. After all, a squirrel is a quick-moving, spunky little animal, and this one was anything but frisky.

Once inside I took one glance around the place and instantly decided there was no way I was going to spend the night there. Sure, Jimmy and I had hoped earlier that his uncle would invite us to stay—that was why we went there in the first place. But after rolling my eyes around that dusky, one-room dwelling there was no way that was going to happen. Other than weak rays of pale, late-day light filtering through two dusty windows, the only other glow in the cave-like structure came from the last flames of an all-but-spent log in the fireplace. Uncle Squirrel's wife, a thin, weary-looking woman turned from a stove on the other side of the room but said nothing. All she did when Jimmy introduced me was nod her head slightly. And I could plainly see that she had dug as deep into her will as she possibly could to offer the small gesture. When I now think back about that woman in her tattered housedress and apron, I can't help but to visualize Dorothea Lange's iconic depression-era, black-and-white photograph—the one with a forlorn, thirty-two-year-old mother holding two of her seven hungry children in front of their ramshackle cabin.

But back inside that Virginia cabin Jimmy's aunt turned back to her antique stove, and I shifted my eyes to the far side of the room—maybe twelve feet away at the most. Three scruffy, but wide-eyed, little children were sitting side by side on the bottom mattress of a wood-framed bunk bed. Again, it was quite dark in there, but with those six inquisitive eyes stretched wide open the way they were, they looked like a trio of startled young owls sitting on a perch. Obviously they hadn't often seen honest-to-goodness, in-the-flesh city-slickers like me and their cousin. Not wanting to gawk at the kids, I soon turned my gaze from them and looked around some more. The furniture was sparse and worn, there was no television, and the large oval area rug in the middle of the wooden floor was threadbare and soiled. Also, the room stunk of lard and whatever it might have been Squirrel's wife was frying in a sizzling fry pan. Even to a teenager who'd grown up with next to nothing, the whole scenario was depressing.

About that time, the portly man in overalls turned to his wife and asked her if there was enough food for "comp-ny." Hearing that, I wasted no time listing my head toward Jimmy next to me and whispering, "No way I'm going to eat *here*, man. Let's split, like right now." He didn't put up an argument.

Squirrel invited us to eat with his family and spend the night as well, but Jimmy promptly and politely turned down his offer. He told him we had already eaten and booked a room at the only motel in the then-small town. And that we only stopped in to say hello. Ten minutes later—a very long ten minutes later, we were on our way. We hadn't even bothered to ask if they had a phone we could use to call for a cab back into town. We knew the answer to that.

It must have been a three-mile trek. Other than the wall of tall trees that seemed to be closing in on both sides of us as the sun dipped to the horizon, all we saw was a rundown country store and small farm across the road from it. Ravenously hungry by now, we climbed the wooden steps into the store and bought a package of sliced baloney, a loaf of bread, and a jar of French's Mustard. After paying for that we marched back across the road, snuck behind the farm's weather-beaten red barn, and slapped mustard on the bread with our plastic combs.

With the food in our stomachs we walked and walked and walked until finally, after the sun had set, a pickup truck came down the road. As if choreographed we both stuck out our thumbs, and the good ole boy behind the wheel was kind enough to give us a lift to the George Washington Motel. The effects of the vodka had long worn off by then, and we were drop-dead exhausted. After paying the motel clerk for a room, we trudged up the stairs, showered, and the last thing I remember is falling onto that bed. I was out like a light before I even landed on it.

When morning came Jimmy and I both woke with splitting headaches and nasty hangovers. Looking like we'd been dragged through the woods behind a log skidder, I asked my best buddy how much money we had left for the trip south. After digging his hand into the pocket of his dirty jeans he pulled out a grand total of seventy-two cents. That was it, less than a buck. But it didn't deter us. We were still dead set on becoming Miami Beach golden boys, and we reaffirmed that we were going the distance. But then I asked him for a dime, so I could call my mother. I knew that if no one else, at least she would be worried about me. But since we were out of cigarettes and only had enough scratch left to buy a pack of Marlboros, Jimmy put up some resistance. I called him an egghead and told him I'd get the damned dime back since I was calling collect.

In a dark phone booth in the back of a dimly-lit Rexall Drugstore that looked as old as the Gettysburg battlefield, I told my mother I was in Virginia. But she was one step ahead of me. She already knew where I was heading. After I hadn't come home from school the previous afternoon, she'd gone to the Brooklyn candy store where Jimmy and I hung out to shake down our friends. One of them eventually weakened, too. Kevin Turley told her that Jimmy had mentioned something about us possibly going to Florida. Once my mom and I got that part of the conversation out of the way she asked me in a desperate tone when I'd be coming back.

"Don't worry, Ma," I told her, "I'll come back to visit in a few months."

"A few months!" she shouted into the phone, her voice more concerned than I'd ever heard it before, *"You can't! You've gotta come home right now!"*

"I can't, Ma. I'm going to Florida. I'll tell you what, though, I'll come back in a few weeks."

Then she sounded downright panicky. With desperate fear framing her every syllable, she pleaded, "Georgie, please! Please come home right now. Don't do this to me." Tough and strong-willed as she had always been, I'd heard her voice breaking up over the line. She was actually crying. I couldn't believe my ears and immediately felt really lousy.

"Alright," I said, looking out the booth's folding glass door at Jimmy futzing around with something he'd taken off a shelf. "I'll come home today. We'll head back right now."

"Do you have enough money for a bus?" she asked, still shook up.

"Yeah," I lied. "Don't worry. We got enough."

"How much do you have?"

Busted now, all I could do was come back in a small sheepish voice, "We got seventy-two cents."

"Seventy-two cents!" she hollered again, *"Are you out of your mind!* But then she calmed down a bit and said, "Okay, listen to me. What's the name of the town

60

you're in? I'll have your father go down to Western Union and wire you the money for two train tickets home."

I told her that we were in Fredericksburg. But instead of taking the train home that day Jimmy and I hopped a Greyhound Bus, because the price of the tickets was much cheaper. With the difference we were able to buy two packs of smokes instead of one and feast on breakfasts and lunches that would have satisfied kings. But despite that, the trip home was far from fun.

The entire way to New York's bustling Port Authority Bus Terminal and on the subway to Brooklyn after that, I was scared to death. I was certain that my old man would give me holy hell for just upping and leaving. But I was wrong. I was shocked by the only thing he said after I walked into our apartment. As if he were talking to somebody in dire need of a frontal lobotomy, he narrowed his eyes, scrunched up his face, and said, "You're a damn fool! Ya shoulda kept going." Then he turned his head and eyes back to the TV and watched the rest of Walter Cronkite's evening news report.

When my mind returned to the here and now it didn't seem possible that all those memories could have freight-trained through my mind in just a few minutes. But they had, and as that last one faded, I took one more glance around the town I hadn't seen in five decades. After taking one more look around, I led Rocky back to the van, thinking how so much had changed in Fredericksburg, Virginia, and how so much had changed in my life. I couldn't believe that fifty years had come and gone so damn quickly and that deeply disturbed me. Right away I tried to shake away

61

the ominous thought, but before I did another crowded right alongside it in the forefront of my mind. It was my age. And as it had many times before, the number 66 seemed like a nagging, intimidating warning. Again, like a dark, violent approaching storm, the reality that I didn't have a whole hell of a lot of time left on this planet haunted my soul.

"Come on Rocky. Let's go," I said in an attempt to shoo away that troubling thought. "We've got to find a store where I can get you a leash and a few other things."

Not far from the gas station I found a PetSmart store. But as I pulled into a parking spot, I realized I had a dilemma on my hands. Dogs were allowed inside their stores but I'd look like some kind of wacko walking him through the aisles on the end of a twenty-five-foot electrical cord. But on the other hand I was really worried about leaving him in the van and out of site for even a minute. Right or wrong I closed all the curtains, put him in back on the mattress, hoped he'd stay there where nobody could see him, and beat heels into the store. Once inside, I rushed up and down the aisles, quickly snatching the things he needed off the shelves. I bought a retractable leash; a harness, since his neck was a long way from being healed; a bag of Kibbles 'n Bits; some salve for his wound; and a bottle of much-needed doggy shampoo. Once I hurried out of the store, you can bet that my eyes were trained on the van. It might seem I was over concerned, but with all the sick, sad stories I'd heard about dogs being stolen, whether it had been for some sicko's personal pet, puppy mill, or a far worse scenario, I was really nervous. So when I climbed into the van and saw Rocky still in the back on the mattress, I was hugely relieved. I opened the bag of Kibbles 'n Bits and gave him a generous amount. After that I drove the short distance to I-95 and merged onto the busy highway, but we didn't get very far before something stopped us in our tracks—almost dead in our tracks.

Chapter 7

Traffic was quite heavy on that stretch of highway leaving Fredericksburg. And everybody was flying. Even though I stayed in the right-hand lane—what's known as the "slow lane," I had to do seventy-five to keep up with everybody else there. I was behind a tractor trailer and though I had no idea why, the driver suddenly sped up as he tried to pull into the next lane. Right before my eyes the truck started to swerve and fishtail uncontrollably. Then things got really ugly. Another eighteen-wheeler had been in front of him, and before the driver I was tailing could successfully make the lane change, he smashed smack into the left side of the other truck.

"Ohhh shhhit!" I cried out so loud that Rocky jumped up on all fours.

I did not want to look at what was going to happen next but had no choice. After shooting a lightning-quick glance out my rearview and back at the road again, I hit the brake pedal—hard. And just as I did both semis began to swerve and slither like two maniacal sixty-foot snakes. Their boxy trailers started swaying side to side, ever so precariously on their suspensions. They looked like they were going to tip any second. To make matters even worse, all three of us were then atop an unbelievably high overpass, and there was another highway full of speeding vehicles beneath it.

Just as the truck drivers surely were, I was in a near panic now. With the A/C on high and windows closed tight I still heard all too clearly the dreadful, drawn out high-pitched squeal of screeching of brakes. At that point I was yanking the wheel this way and that, fighting to keep control of the van. And I could smell burning rubber from the tires of both trucks blowing in my dashboard vents along with cool, air-conditioned air. Then it got worse yet. The two trucks hit the railing—first the lead one, then the one behind it.

"Oh my God! No!" I screamed out, stretching out the no, crunching down even harder on the brake pedal.

Having all I could do to stay out of the lane next to mine I flung my right arm to the side, holding Rocky back the best I could. I thought for sure we were going to smash into the behemoth in front of me. Then, right in the middle of all this chaos, a vision flashed through my mind. I could see the van sliding beneath the enormous truck—and me being decapitated. *"Hold on Rocky!"* I screamed, as we skidded along the asphalt for what seemed like forever.

Finally we stopped, and I felt my heart doing an entirely different dance than it ever had before—BADDA-BOOM BADDA-BING BADDA-BOOM-BOOM-BING—it pounded.

I thought for sure my screwed up ticker was going to burst clear through its ribbed cage. All around me, like a flock of frenetic two-ton bats, cars slid on the roadway and brakes squealed. When the two out-of-control big rigs had slammed into the guardrail, sections of both their trailers had splayed into the adjacent lane, and all the drivers were now trying to avoid them.

What I witnessed next was as close to a miracle as I'd ever seen. Despite all the traffic rushing up all the lanes, not a single vehicle hit the wrecked trucks. And when I tell you that I had finally come to a stop within two feet of the truck in front of me, I kid you not. But there was no time to think about that. I had to act and act fast.

With my heart still caroming off the inside of my ribs fast as a high-speed piston I jumped out of the van, slamming the door behind me so Rocky couldn't jump out onto the chaotic highway. Then I shot one look back at the oncoming traffic, sprinted alongside the closest truck, leapt onto the first steel step outside its fuel tank, grabbed onto the Mack truck's boarding handle and yanked myself up the second step. The driver's side window was still intact but badly shattered. With so many crisscrossing cracks the Plexiglas looked like the web of an overworked spider, and I couldn't see inside too well. Only when I rose on my toes and looked in through the very top of the window, was I able to see the thirtyish, Asian-American man inside, and he did not look good. With the trunk of his body bent towards the passenger seat— tilted over it sideways in a very unnatural position, I knew he had broken his back. But that wasn't all. Blood was splattered all over the inside of the cab, and streams of it were pulsating out of the side of his head—right through his black hair. What was propelling the red discharges were the final beats of the unfortunate man's heart.

"My good Lord," I muttered, yanking on the door's handle with all I had. But it wouldn't open. That was it. There was nothing I could do for the dying man.

Giving up at that point, I spun my head around to check the traffic coming up from behind. It was already crawling. That quickly the other three northbound lanes had backed up. Every passing motorist and their passengers were rubbernecking.

I jumped down from the truck's steps, and as I dashed from the rear to the front of the next one, I couldn't believe what I was seeing. The monstrous enclosed trailer was bent in the middle like a jackknife. I saw that the truck's cab had broken clear through the guard rail. It was now hanging over the high overpass, just dangling there, a hundred feet above the highway below.

Unable to see the driver from where I was, I climbed atop the barrier, leaned my knees against the railing above it, and looked down through the driver's side window. This time there was something moving inside the cab. I saw the top of the dazed trucker's head, slowly swaying from side to side. But what could I do? I couldn't very well leap over the guardrail, grab a hold of the door handle, and try to yank the thing open. Such a precarious attempt would have been insane.

It was then that I heard a woman's voice.

"I just called 911," she shouted out her car's open window. "They're on their way."

Finally coming to my senses, I glanced down at the cars and trucks racing beneath the overpass and carefully got down from my perch atop the concrete barrier.

"That's good," I said to the middle-aged lady wearing a business suit. "Maybe they can do something for this poor guy. I'm afraid it's too late to help the other driver though. I just checked on him and he's all but gone. He's bleeding badly. All I can say is thank God he's unconscious."

"What a disaster," the woman said, as the mammoth engine inside the dangling cab continued to hiss. "I hope to God it doesn't fall. It looks like it could let go any second."

"Shhh," I said then. "Listen. I think I hear sirens."

They were coming from way down the clogged highway. And after the woman and I turned toward the sound in unison, we saw flashing blue lights slowly weaving through the mess.

"There's no sense in you being tied up here," I told her. "There's nothing you can do. I'll have to hang around a while and tell the police what happened. I was right behind the trucks when they crashed. The one in back hit the other and forced him to lose control."

The lady said, "You're right." She took one more look at the small section of the blue cab that was visible, flashed the sign of the cross with her right hand and drove away slowly.

By now it was getting downright hot out so I hurried back to the van to check on Rocky. I turned the engine over and A/C on again and stayed with him until the authorities worked their way up to the wreck. Once they did, I told them what I had seen, they filled out a report, then they halted all the endless lines of traffic so I could pull the van out from behind the wreckage and be on my way.

As Rocky and I headed for Maryland, where I figured we'd spend the night, I stroked his head for a while and pondered what I had taken away from the gruesome collision. I thought about how most people so rarely give thought to just how precarious our human existence actually is. Certainly when the two drivers involved in that terrible accident were putting on their pants that morning, neither of them had a clue that something so horrific was going to happen to them. We just never know. Sure, in some ways it's good that it is not our nature to dwell on such things. But on the other hand, it wouldn't hurt to sometimes remind ourselves that our own fate, and that of our loved ones, is in many ways similar to the fate of a tightrope walker. Think about it, if one of those daredevils were to walk a wire high above the Grand Canyon or tethered to two cloud-scratching, big-city skyscrapers, they'd be at the mercy of factors they couldn't control. Even if they walked the straight and narrow wire perfectly, who's to say a rogue wind might not suddenly appear out of nowhere? What if one of The Flying Wallendas was doing the tall building thing in Frisco or L.A. when an earthquake happened to occur? Would it be a long shot? Sure. But the lead driver in the accident I had just witnessed would've told you the same thing about the odds of him getting slammed off a highway and finding himself hanging over a guardrail. The other driver—the one I found out had died before I'd left the scene—he sure as hell hadn't thought when he rolled out of bed that morning that it was going to be his last time. We simply cannot allow ourselves to take our lives for granted.

When I myself had awoken one morning when in my mid-thirties, I'd had no clue that on that particular day I'd be knocked down by lightning while pier fishing beneath a clear blue sky. Talk about long odds! Granted, a thin line of evil, ink-blue clouds had just begun to peek over the distant horizon. But it was exactly that—the thinnest of narrow bands—barely visible and so far off in the distance behind us fishermen that we didn't know it existed. Even as cautious about such things as I'd always been, if I had seen it I still wouldn't have made a mad dash off that pier. Sure, I'd have kept an eye on it, but I never would have dreamed such a powerful bolt of lightning could come from such a thin line of clouds so far away. But it did, and it struck the concrete fishing pier just thirty feet away from me—at the very spot I had been standing only minutes earlier.

No, not all of us will end up in a hospital bed knowing that our final hour is approaching. For some of us there will be no warning. Look at me, when I had set out on my road trip I certainly knew I had health issues. I also knew, all too well, that I was far from immortal; that the end of my sixty-six-year journey could be just around the bend of any road I might take. Between knowing those things, being so darned glad to have finally broken out of my Florida imprisonment, and witnessing the carnage I just had seen outside of Fredericksburg, my mind was made up, I was going to have the time of my life. No matter how much or how little time I might have left, I was now going to make sure I enjoyed it. And I was determined to make sure my fuzzy new companion did as well. After all, Lord only knew what he had been through.

Chapter 8

Rocky and I spent our first night together in gorgeous Patapsco Valley State Park, outside of Baltimore, Maryland. I quit driving early, and as soon as I pulled the van into our campsite and hooked up the water and electricity, I gave him a complete makeover. I hosed him down and shampooed him not once but twice. He was that dirty. But he cleaned up really well and seemed to feel much better. Once I dried him off, had we been back in 1938, he looked so spiffy he could have given Toto (a fellow Cairn Terrier) some serious competition for the part of Dorothy's dog in *The Wizard of Oz*.

The next day was my third on the road, and I drove more hours than I'd planned. When Rocky and I set out before dawn, I knew that getting through Baltimore that early wouldn't be a problem. But I dreaded fighting my way up the New Jersey Turnpike and later through New York City. Once I got close to New York, I decided I definitely did not want to deal with driving into Manhattan. Instead, I took the Verrazano Bridge from Staten Island into Brooklyn. Once we made our way through that borough and then through Queens, I picked up the Long Island Expressway and headed farther east.

Although New Yorkers call the Long Island Expressway "The world's longest parking lot," I got lucky that afternoon. Traffic wasn't bad at all, and the further we got from the city, the more the stream of traffic thinned out. Had it been only an hour later we would definitely have gotten stuck in rush hour traffic, when it crawls slower than a bad weather funeral procession. But it wasn't all smooth sailing. By the time we neared the Coram exit, the entire sky was a dreary, dishtowel gray. A light rain began to fall, and as it did a tear dripped from one of my eyelashes and fell on my cheek. I was all too familiar with this stretch of highway. I had driven on it countless times during the thirty years Lorna and I had lived on Long Island. You see, the home we had shared was in the town of Port Jefferson, just a few miles away from where I was now.

"I love you honey and always will," I said, when I approached the sign for Exit 64 Coram - our old exit.

And as I was driving by it a moment later, the rain started pouring down hard at the exact same time I glanced down that road. Visibility was near zero, but through the rain-streaked window I could still make out *Capriotti's Ristorante. Capriotti's* was the place that Lorna and I had gone to so many times over the years to celebrate special occasions. Immediately then, visions of some of those happy times flashed through my mind. But I didn't get to see too many visions because before they stopped coming. For as I took two more quick looks out my driver's side window, the restaurant beneath that overcast sky didn't look much like the happy place it once had been. It looked dark, forlorn. It also appeared extremely blurry now. And that wasn't only because of all the streaks of gray rain streaming down the glass I was looking through. I was actually crying—crying hard. And my heart was doing that clumsy uncertain dance inside my chest.

It wasn't until a couple of miles after I'd passed *Capriotti's* that my sobs began to subside. As they did, I gently wiped my damp eyes with my fingertips and noticed something out of the corner of my right eye. It was a movement. It was Rocky. And although he, too, appeared blurry, I could plainly see that he had sat up.

My new pet was looking at me—staring right into my eyes as if he were reading what was going on behind them. He was sad. The way his eyes drooped, he looked concerned. There was no doubt, he was worried about me. Granted, over a period of time many dogs begin to sense things about their owners, but this was different. I was sure Rocky had never interacted much with people. Both the welt around his neck and his scrawny, undernourished body were evidence of that. Yet here was this dog I had not even spent two full days with, sympathizing with me. It was then that I realized I had a very special animal sitting by my side.

As I sniffled one last time, I rested the palm of my hand atop his little head. "Well," I said, "I'll be a son of a gun, Rockster. You truly feel bad for me. Don't you?"

As I petted his head I well knew it wasn't only my gentle strokes that caused his eyes to brighten and his tail to wag. It was also the grateful smile on my face.

"You are one smart pup, aren't you? You knew I was unhappy. You really knew and you cared."

As if to say, "Yes! Yes!" his stubby tail wagged faster. It was flapping back and forth faster than the high-speed wipers on the windshield. His breathing escalated to a rapid succession of short pants, too, and the way his mouth opened slightly, it looked as though he was smiling. I was really beginning to bond Rocky. He amazed me. Knowing that he had actually pulled me out of a potential deep funk made the smile on my face stretch even wider. And it stayed that way as I drove on with my hand resting on my new companion's furry back.

A short time later we exited the expressway, picked up Route 25 and continued further east. That quiet two-lane road would take us to the end of Long Island's quaint North Fork, where the village of Orient Point sat on the easternmost tip of it. It was at Orient Point that Steinbeck had kicked off his cross-country trip in 1960. In all reality, his journey actually had begun when he left his home in nearby Sag Harbor, but it was at Orient that he drove his custom-made camper onto a ferry and headed to New London, Connecticut.

Along with his poodle Charley the Nobel Laureate crossed Long Island Sound just like Rocky and I were going to do the next morning. Although the famous author had done it shortly after Labor Day I was doing it about a week before Memorial Day. But that didn't matter. I couldn't help believing that I was every bit as excited as he must have been - no matter what time of year it was. Granted, we both were getting up in age when we embarked on our respective trips, and we both had health issues. But just as Steinbeck had, I wanted to become reacquainted with America and its people. Sure, I had left Florida with low expectations for both, but after three days on the road, and meeting some of the people I already had encountered, my hopes for what I might find out there were now improving.

As Rocky and I drove along that same stretch of country road Steinbeck had a half century earlier, the sun broke through the clouds. And as we passed through small villages with American Indian names like Aquebogue, Mattituck, and Cutchogue, the late-afternoon sky brightened and became bluer. By the time Cutchogue was disappearing in my rearview mirror, the wind picked up. The weather suddenly became blustery and the wind was coming out of the north. The temperature suddenly dropped about fifteen degrees in minutes. Obviously, the rain we'd had earlier had been brought on by an approaching front pushing its way south across Long Island Sound.

"Ah, Rocky," I said after switching off the A/C and rolling my window down, "do you feel this air? I had a feeling a cool front might be moving in."

Despite being road weary after driving all the way from Maryland, the refreshing sea air gave me a second wind of sorts. I was so glad to be out of hot, muggy Florida and I wished I never had to go back. But I quickly put the skids on the latter thought. I wasn't going to worry about that now. Florida could sink back in the ocean as far as I was concerned. There were adventures waiting down the road and I was going to savor every single one of them.

"Okay good boy," I said to Rocky, "we're almost at the campground." And as soon as those words left my mouth, I'll be damned if he didn't sit right up and start that contented panting again.

Earlier that day, when we were on the Jersey Turnpike, I'd pulled into a rest stop to check my Good Sam Club Directory. And after seeing that one campground was located just a few miles from Orient Point, I walked Rocky across the sprawling parking lot to a payphone and reserved a site. Of course, since I'd gotten the telephone-book-thick directory a few years earlier—when Lorna and I still dreamed together about doing the cross-country trip—the rates at all the campgrounds had been cheaper. By now all the rates listed had risen considerably. And the few campgrounds on the Eastern tip of Long Island were not exceptions. None were cheap by any means. But as far as they were out of my reach, I had no other choice but to splurge this time. The best deal I could find was in the historic seaport of Greenport, so I ended up reserving a site there.

At about 4 PM Rocky and I pulled into that campground. It certainly was nice enough. And it was clear to see that lots of other people must have thought so. Most of the sites were already occupied and there was lots of activity going on. In front of many of the RVs, travel trailers, and tents, children were at play. And their parents were either barbecuing or taking life easy in lawn chairs. With sprawling Peconic Bay on one side of the grounds and the attractive village of Greenport nearby to shop, dine, or just plain knock around in, I could see why so many families came to stay. But I wasn't looking for action. After nine hours on the road all I wanted to do was take a shower, feed Rocky, and put some more of the salve I'd bought on the nasty gash around his neck. After doing all that, I sat outside the van, popped open a beer, and smoked my eighth cigarette of the day.

Before falling into a deep sleep that night, my ticker only flip-flopped twice. The accompanying squeezes in my chest had been slight, barely discernible now, and I was beginning to allow myself to believe that the only thing causing the irregularities was stress. I wanted so badly to be right. But before dozing off that nagging conflicting side of my psyche muscled its way into my thoughts again, insisting I was full of bunk and that there *was* definitely something wrong with me, something *seriously* wrong. But I fought back. I refused to let such dark negativity dim the new light that finally, after three years, had found its way into my spirit.

"No!" I insisted aloud into the darkness, "I am not going to let this happen. I'm going to keep thinking positively."

But that wasn't quite the end of it. *If I'm wrong,* I thought, *so be it. If and when the big one hits, I'll probably be gone in no time anyway. I'll probably be in pain and panic for a few seconds, but . . . .*

Right there I forced myself to halt the frightful thought. I shoved the whole shooting match out of my head. After finally feeling better about my life, for three consecutive days, I wasn't about to let my mind revert back to the dungeon of dark thoughts where it had lingered too long. Instead, I rolled over onto my side, slid my hand beneath my pillow, and said goodnight to Lorna. After that, as if on cue, little Rocky backed up snug against my chest. Gently I laid my free arm over him. I smiled once again, and in no time at all, we both drifted off into a contented, restful sleep.

It was chilly in the van that night and not much warmer when we woke up in the predawn darkness. But that was fine by me. I pulled a clean black sweatshirt over my head, slid into a pair of blue jeans, and relished the cool weather all over again. I was still mighty happy to be out of the muggy Florida heat.

Rocky and I had plenty of bounce in our steps when I took him out to do his morning business. Once that was accomplished I had my instant coffee and morning smoke outside. After that I fed my partner and myself. He had his second meal out of the new bag of Kibbles 'n Bits, and I cooked myself a Boca Burger and toasted two slices of whole wheat bread. Being the flexitarian I was, albeit somewhat loosely-disciplined at times, vegetarian burgers were fine by me. With a light smear of margarine on the toast, I felt like I was eating a sausage sandwich.

For the next few hours we took it easy that fine morning. We knocked around the campground a bit and strolled through downtown Greenport. After that we drove the short distance to Orient Point and boarded the 10 AM ferry to New London. Not long after it left the dock I got a hankering for more coffee. I saw a lady come out of the snack bar with a piping-hot cup in hand, and when she walked by me, that was it. One whiff of the freshly-brewed stuff and I was craving it. But there was a snag. Dogs weren't allowed inside the enclosed areas. All I could do was hope somebody would walk by where I was sitting on the deck and be kind enough to watch Rocky for a minute or so. As I waited for a likely Samaritan, I looked out at Long Island Sound. Because that cool front had passed through the previous afternoon there was virtually no wind now. The water was slick calm, too, but not much of it was visible. A dense fog, gray as the water surrounding the ferry, hadn't yet lifted, making it impossible to see to more than fifty yards out from where I sat behind the railing.

Rocky and I were only there a minute or so when a man considerably older than me came walking up the deck toward us. He appeared to be about eighty years old, but he had a full head of white hair neatly parted on the side and looked to be full of vigor. Quite thin and dressed in casual, yet expensive clothes, he walked with the easy, confident gait of a medieval lord. By the logo monogrammed on the breast pocket of his blue oxford shirt, the sharp pleat in his chinos, and the shiny high-quality loafers on his feet, I could tell he was a man who had never worried about balancing a monthly budget. The Wall Street Journal folded beneath his arm only seemed to confirm my evaluation.

"Howdy!" he said in a tone every bit as self-assured as his walk—too confident for my liking.

Nodding my head I said, "Good morning," in a cordial tone, though I hoped he'd keep walking. But he didn't. Limber as a man half his age, he stopped walking, squatted down alongside Rocky and held out his hand for him to sniff.

"Ruff! Ruff! Ruff, ruff, ruff!" Rocky barked. But his tone wasn't aggressive and he started wagging his tail.

"Well, well. It's okay big boy," the octogenarian said as calmly as could be.

Then with his hand remaining perfectly still, he raised his eyes to me and asked, "Is it okay to pet him?"

"Well . . . sure. His name's Rocky. Just be careful not to touch his neck. Beneath his fur he's got a nasty gash."

Lowering his eyes back to Rocky he softly petted the top of his head.

"Oh, really? What happened to you Rocky?" he asked, still looking at him but obviously directing the question to me. But since the man's tone didn't sound overly suspicious, I didn't take a whole lot of offense.

Leaning over a bit, putting my elbows to my knees I told him, "I found him a few mornings ago, in North Carolina. He had either broken away from his owners or they'd abandoned him. The gash encircles his entire neck. I would imagine whoever owned him left a collar on him long after he'd outgrown it."

"Hmmm," he said, "let me take a look here."

"Be careful. It's very tender."

Before proceeding he looked up at me. With his forehead furrowed the way it was, I could tell he was genuinely concerned. With his mouth then pulling into a small knowing smile, he told me, "Don't worry. For fifty-two years I treated everything from gerbils to giraffes. I'm a retired veterinarian."

"No kidding, really?"

"Yupper. I kid you not," he said, leaning toward Rocky, ever so gently separated the tawny fur on his neck.

I couldn't help liking the old guy, and that surprised me. All my life I'd never had any great love for the well-to-do. Not when so many people like me always had to struggle to make ends meet. No, it had nothing to do with being jealous. I never gave a hoot about having a lot of *things* anyway. All I'd ever wanted was enough to get by, without having any financial worries. But year after year that had become increasingly more difficult. And while things continued to get tougher for people like me and Lorna, most of Corporate America's biggest shareholders had raked in more and more money, at the expense of those who'd struggled. But that wasn't first and foremost on my mind now as this man inspected Rocky. I could see that no matter how much wealth he might have had, he also had a heart. And I wholeheartedly appreciated what he was doing.

"He was filthy when I found him alongside a highway. I cleaned him up the best I could that night and have been applying a salve ever since."

"Well . . . keep doing what you're doing," he said while carefully finger-combing Rocky's fur back over the cut.

Still crouched down there, he gave him a quick once over. He checked his teeth, gums, eyes, ears and paws. He also felt around his stomach and ribs before telling me that my partner seemed quite healthy. And that the wound looked like it was beginning to heal nicely.

"My name's George, George McLast," I said, extending my hand. "Thanks very much for taking a look at him."

Standing up then he said, "No problem. It's a pleasure to meet you," and as we shook hands he added, "I'm Fred Dahlstrom. And I definitely agree with you about what caused Rocky's wound. It had to be from a restraint he'd outgrown. But since he looks to be about five or six years old, and the gash is so wide, I don't think it was a collar. I'm thinking there was a chain around his neck. Most collars wouldn't last for that long a time, particularly if he had always been left outdoors in all kinds of weather."

We both noticed then that two pretty young ladies were coming toward us. Since there wasn't much space between the bench and the ferry's railing, I pulled my feet closer in and Fred stepped to the side so they could pass. As the laughing, seemingly-carefree girls passed by us, Doctor Dahlstrom looked back at me and devilishly wiggled his eyebrows a couple of times. But he quickly became more serious.

"As calloused as Rocky's paw pads are," he said, "I'm afraid to say I think he very well might have spent his days tied to a tree outside. You've probably seen that sad scenario—a dog tethered to a tree trunk with a circular dirt path worn through the grass around it."

"You've got to be kidding!" I came back, outraged now, visualizing the sweet little animal lying at my feet tied up in such a way, in all kinds of weather.

"What in God's name is wrong with some of these sub humans?"

As if we might find the answer to my question in the expansive waters surrounding us, we both turned our heads and eyes out towards Long Island Sound. The fog was thinning and as the ferry chugged forward, the sun broke through what was left of it.

"I just don't know," the vet said, our gaze shifting to two seagulls flying right alongside the boat. Fifty feet out from the railing at most; flapping their wings slowly, they seemed to be keeping time with the bulky craft intentionally as if escorting it.

"I've seen hundreds and hundreds of abused animals during the years I practiced," Fred said, as we continued to watch the white birds, "and never once could I emotionally detach myself from a single one of them."

I glanced down at Rocky in silence for a moment then looked back at the vet asking, "How in the hell could he have ever gotten a *chain* off his neck? God, I don't like to even think about it. It's so damn inhumane."

"That's a good question. Maybe a neighbor or somebody else saw him tied up like that day after day. Maybe they finally got fed up with it. They could have waited until the owners left their house one day and freed him by cutting the damn thing off. Who knows for sure? The fortunate thing is that he hooked up with you. The wound's not infected and it's beginning to heal."

There was another short pause in our conversation. The length of the ferry was undulating up and down now, making its way across the wake of a freighter that had passed in front of it. When it smoothed out a few seconds later, I asked, "Listen, Fred, could you hang onto Rocky's leash for a minute or two while I run inside here to get a cup of coffee? I'm dying for one, and they don't allow pets in the snack bar."

"No problem at all. I'll be glad to," he said reaching for the leash.

"Can I get you one?" I asked as I rose to my feet.

"Sure. Why not? Black no sugar would be fine."

When I came back outside minutes later and handed Fred one of the Styrofoam cups, we continued to talk. We conversed for what was left of the hour-and-twenty-minute ride to New London. He told me that he lived in Westport, Connecticut. Though I had never actually been in the town, I'd passed by the exit to it on I-95 a few times over the years. And I very well knew it was a big-bucks area. I once read somewhere that when Paul Newman was alive he and his wife Joanne Woodward had called Westport home for many years. Fred also went on to tell me that he had just spent three days with his sister at her summer place in Greenport. She obviously had money as well.

Fred and I had an interesting conversation and it flowed easily. It turned out that despite our socio-economic and age differences, Fred and I had quite a bit in common. We talked about a lot of things, shared a few laughs, and seemed to view life in a similar perspective. By the time he told me about some of his college day escapades at Dartmouth back in the late 1940's and 50's, I began to feel that had we met earlier in life, he and I could very well have become lifelong friends. It didn't seem to matter that he'd come from an old-money family and grown up in Westport. I liked the guy. And this wasn't the first time on the trip that one of my predetermined beliefs escaped the box it had been locked inside for a long time. I still believed, and would continue to do so for whatever time I had left, that the increasingly unfair spread of wealth in America was responsible for the downfall of its working class. But meeting Fred Dahlstrom did make me realize something I had always preferred to doubt. And that was that even though some people do financially well in what I saw as an unbalanced system, it doesn't mean they don't care about those less fortunate.

During the entire crossing Rocky had been perfectly content to simply lie down quietly on the metal deck while we talked. He was still catching up on his much-needed rest. After all, God only knew how long he'd been on the loose in North Carolina and what he'd gone through. He didn't get up once until we approached the New London dock, when we men stood up, stepped over to the railing, and watched the vessel pull into its birth.

"Well," Fred said, as the ferry's engines slowed to idling speed, "are you going to stop at one of the casinos? You know they're just a short ride from here, don't you?"

"Sure, I know. But I really shouldn't be gambling right now. I've got to be sure we have enough money for the long trip ahead." Then looking down at Rocky standing alongside my ankle, I added, "Even if I said the hell with it and decided to play the slots for an hour or so, I've got my new buddy with me. As much as I'm tempted it's out of the question."

"Heck, George, you can park near the RV parking at Foxwoods. You said your van has curtains on all the windows. And one that slides closed behind the front seats. It's cool out today, Rocky would be fine in there. Plus, the casinos have security guards who constantly patrol the lot. You should go. Have yourself a good time."

I couldn't believe what happened next. Fred's last words had barely left his mouth when he reached into his back pocket for his wallet.

"Here, take this," he said, extracting two, one-hundred-dollar bills and holding them out towards me, "Have some fun."

I could have gotten angry at him. A lot of men would have been insulted by such a gesture, particularly men my age. Some would have felt it was demeaning, a blow to their pride. I could have taken it that way, too. But unusual as the offering was, I didn't take it that way. I took it as what Fred meant it to be—simply a token of his kindness. But I did not take his money.

With a heartfelt appreciative smile on my face, I waved a hand at it saying, "Aw, Fred, that's awfully kind of you. But I couldn't. Rocky and I have a lot more miles to drive today. I'm hoping to get up to Deer Isle, Maine by dinnertime. But hey, thank you very much anyway."

My new unlikely friend understood. He put the money back in his wallet and jotted his telephone number in a small notebook he had in his shirt pocket. Pulling the page out of it and handing it to me, he told me that if I was ever in the Westport area, to give him a call. I appreciated that gesture as well, but as I folded the paper in half and put it in the pocket of my jeans I was sure I'd never use it. A minute or two later the ferry docked; we shook hands and went our separate ways.

About twenty minutes later with Rocky sitting on his hind legs alongside me watching the world rush by through the passenger window, we drove by the Foxwoods exit on Interstate 395. As we did Fred Dahlstrom's compassionate face reappeared in my mind, and I found myself smiling again.

Chapter 9

The hour drive up I-395 was a peaceful one. There was very little traffic, and I was quite impressed with the beauty of Eastern Connecticut. Beneath a clear, azure sky, the forests and rolling landscape were bursting with the bright, vivid colors of autumn, and I could easily see how somebody would want to call the area home. I would have loved to get off the highway and look around a little. I'd have killed, well, almost killed, to buy a small home and settle down in such a place. But I knew that to even entertain such a thought would be a pipedream. Like I said earlier I could never again afford to buy a place in the Northeast United States, and as I drove on that realization irked me as it had so many other times since Lorna and I had moved to Florida. Once again the same all-too-familiar feelings of regret and failure twisted inside my stomach. They continued their wrenching until Rocky and I got off that scenic stretch of highway. And as soon as we did the quiet, peaceful ambience quickly changed. Things other than my remorse demanded my attention.

The fifty-six miles of I-495 we drove through Massachusetts after that was a whole different story. The entire time I kept both hands so tight on the steering wheel that my knuckles were as white as the occasional clouds that scooted by high overhead. Like Connecticut, there were still lots of trees and color alongside the highway. But there were many more lanes on this highway and the traffic was a living nightmare. Cars, busses, trucks, vans and SUVs were everywhere, and all of them were flying. I was doing a little over seventy, but it seemed like the entire world was zooming by me. Then after that, as much as I had wanted to get to New Hampshire, the short drive through that state was even worse. There were five or six lanes going in both directions on that stretch of I-95, and everybody driving in them was in as big a hurry to get wherever they were going as the motorists back in Massachusetts had been. Fortunately, the madness would soon end.

After passing through Portsmouth and forking over more money for yet another toll, Rocky and I ascended the Piscataqua River Bridge. About the time we got to the middle of the lofty structure, way high above the river, two thoughts crowded into my head at once. From my past readings I had once learned that after a border dispute between Maine and New Hampshire, the Supreme Court had ruled in 2001 that the border between the two states was right where I was—smack in the middle of the bridge. I also remembered reading that when the bridge was under construction in 1977, four unfortunate workers had fallen to their deaths on the Kittery, Maine side of the bridge. But those facts instantly vacated my mind as soon as I reached the other side of the bridge and spied a blue sign with white lettering up ahead on the road's shoulder. Since my eyes weren't what they used to be it at first appeared fuzzy, but as I rolled closer it soon became perfectly clear. It read, Welcome to Maine – The Way Life Should Be. And for once the greeting wasn't just another state blowing its own hollow horn. Sure, Maine, like all the rest, hoped to trump up tourism with their catchy phrase, but even though I had just entered the "Pine Tree State," I already felt far different than I did back in Massachusetts and New Hampshire, and that feeling had nothing to do with the highway here being lined with towering pines instead of broadleaf trees.

Granted, this stretch of I-95 wasn't narrow either, it had four lanes on each side of the median, but there was an immediate change in the ambience. Yes, there still was traffic but far less of it. And almost all the drivers had slowed down considerably. Without even trying to, I found myself beginning to relax. My shoulders had been tight and all hunched up during the previous hour, but by the time Rocky and I approached the very first exit in Kittery, all the tenseness had subsided. Never in my life had I been in Maine. I'd just rolled over the border for the first time minutes earlier, but already I sensed there was something special about the place. I got this tranquil feeling, this sense that this was where I belonged. It was as if a sweet distant voice, a women's voice, was whispering in my ear, "You should have come here a long, long time ago. You would have loved it." Yes, I know, it sounds crazy. But I was already that enamored with the state.

About forty minutes after crossing that bridge, we breezed right through Portland. And from what I could see of Maine's largest city, it looked really nice. Back when I was growing up in New York I loved "The Big Apple," but by now I was no longer a big fan of cities. As I tooled through Portland, though, I could see it wasn't too, too big. It actually looked inviting. Off to the right of the highway I could see an attractive, unimposing skyline next to a wide bay. On the opposite side there were small businesses, unobtrusive homes, and a sprawling green park. After passing the latter we drove a tad further, just north of the city limits, and things slowed down even more. The moderate traffic almost immediately thinned out so much that you could almost call it sparse. Then something else dawned on me. I realized I hadn't seen a single billboard since crossing the state line. I didn't know then that Maine had banned those unsightly eyesores.

A short time later, after passing the quaint town of Freeport where L.L. Bean has a huge store and its corporate headquarters, we exited I-95 into the quaint town of Brunswick. From there we continued north on U.S. 202 and U.S. 1 for an hour and a half. A short time later when it was getting close to 5 PM, I started getting hunger pangs, and it had gotten quite cold. But the timing was just right. Just as I rolled my window closed, I spotted an old, silver-walled diner just up the road. The way it looked, sitting behind its unpaved parking lot and surrounded by trees, I felt like I had returned to the 1960s.

"Rocky," I said, after turning into the nearly deserted parking lot and shutting off the van's engine, "I'm going to be just a little while. If you're a good boy I'll bring you back something nice." Then, road weary and stiff as a corpse, I made my way to the glass door, leaned on it and stepped inside.

The row of ceiling fans overhead was motionless. The stools at the pale green Formica counter, as well as the booth seats along the front windows, looked every bit as old as the outside of the place. But they, too, were immaculate. At one of the booths a man and woman about my age slowly and silently ate meatloaf dinners. The man, dressed in faded denim overalls and a red flannel shirt, was much heavier than me. The white-haired lady across from him also had on blue overalls, and seeing the two of them dressed like that, despite the color difference in their garb, put me to mind of Captain Kangaroo's good-old-boy sidekick, Mister Green Jeans. Sitting at the counter, two men, dressed just as casually, were also digging into their meals. Also with their backs to me, there were two women standing behind the long counter. One of them seemed to be pulling double duty. A stout girl, with a small tattoo of something I couldn't discern on the back of her neck, she had on a waitress's white uniform but was scraping the griddle. The other lady, who was quite shapely, was replenishing the supply of small boxes of breakfast cereal up on a shelf. I couldn't stop myself from giving her a second look. She wasn't very tall, maybe five-five at the most, but with that curvy figure and her black hair meticulously cut where it met her shoulders Cleopatra style, I just knew she had to be a looker.

Finished scoping things out by then, I walked down the narrow aisle to the booth directly in front of where I had nosed the van to the diner. As I sat down and slid to the center of the wide cushy seat, I glanced out the window and gave the Rockster a little wave and a big smile. Already watching me with his paws to the dashboard, I couldn't see his stubby tail, but I knew he was wagging to beat the band.

Turning to the laminated paper menu before me, I immediately saw that the prices were more than fair. It took me a while, but after deciding what to order I again looked toward the two women behind the counter. Both of them had turned around and I could now see that the waitress/cook was young and on the plain side. But the other one, wow, she was something else. Not a kid for sure but still a rare beauty. Dressed in snug, form-fitting jeans that looked new and a turtleneck sweater black as her hair, she had alluring blue eyes that were absolutely mesmerizing—and they were locked on me. Obviously not wanting her tantalizing lips to be read, she tilted her head sideways toward the waitress, lifted her hand in front of her mouth, and whispered something. Then the waitress rolled her eyes toward me, too, and both of them giggled mischievously.

Feeling as awkward as a sixth-grade boy who just got a note from the prettiest girl in the class saying she wanted to kiss him after school, I quickly turned away.

Snatching the menu up again, I trained my eyes on it but couldn't decipher a word of it.

Why in the world is she staring at me like that? She can't be more than forty or forty-five. I've got at least twenty years on her, and geez, what a knockout she is. Okay, Rover, that's it. Calm down and get serious with yourself. Just order your food and forget about it.

Feeling my knees bouncing beneath the table like they sometimes did when I got super nervous, hating myself for it, I put the brakes on them and lowered the menu back on the table.

What the heck? When is the darn waitress coming over here to take my order? This is weird.

Then it got weirder yet. Shooting another glance back over there, I saw that their smiles had stretched even wider. I also saw the waitress pull a yellow pencil from behind her ear and hand it over to Cleopatra, along with her order pad.

This is insane. I thought as I turned away, looked out the window again, saw my image in the glass and finger-combed my hair one time.

Oh stop, idiot. She's not interested in you. I can imagine what she must have said—surely some bumpkin talk about the lonesome-looking stranger passing through town. Hell, they made me feel like I'd grown a second nose out of the top of my head. But on the other hand, why would she take the pad and pencil from the waitress? No, you're out of my head. Quit thinking that nonsense.

Seeing the woman coming by now, I ended my internal monologue with: *Okay! Here she comes! Get your act together, man.*

"Hi there," she said with a smile but not sounding nearly as confident as I thought she would.

Up close now, noticing how her straight white teeth glistened, I answered in as casual a tone as I could muster, "Yes, I ah . . . I'd like the fried flounder with French fries and coleslaw." Then glancing out the window alongside me and pointing to Rocky who was still up on his hind legs, I added, "I'll also need something for my partner out there. Is it possible to get a just one piece of chicken to go for him, maybe a thigh?"

She, too, glanced out at Rocky before turning her eyes back to mine. And with that smile widening she asked, "How about a nice beef patty without a roll? I'll bet he or she would love that."

"He's a he, but no thank you." I came back, squirming in my seat a bit, "I'm not too big on red meat, if you know what I mean."

"Hmmm," she came back, exaggeratedly narrowing her eyes at me and pursing those to-die-for glossy lips, "I see, looks like we have a flexitarian here."

"Well," I said, tilting my head with a little smile of my own, "I'm not exactly a flexitarian. That's someone who's a vegetarian but cheats once in a while. I'm not quite there yet. If something swims or flies I'll eat it, but I stay away from red meat and pork."

She delved deeper into my eyes then, and I thought I might actually be blushing. Immediately I hated myself for reacting like a goofy, bashful teenager. Feeling as if I'd just had my pants pulled down, that smile on my face began to fade.

As if she knew exactly what I was thinking and feeling, this woman said, "Okay, I'll tell you what. What do you say I put some nice hot chicken *tenders* in a bag for your pal? Guaranteed, he'll like them."

"Sure. Fair enough. That sounds good."

"I'll have it for you in a jiffy," she said before turning around. And as she did her eyes lingered on mine a second longer—the way women often do when trying to get a message across.

I couldn't stop myself from watching her as she strode toward the break in the counter. After she got there I couldn't help jumping all over myself either.

I don't know if she's just being friendly, or there's more to her friendliness than meets the eye. Either way, though, I feel guilty as hell thinking about such things. After all the years Lorna and I loved each other, would it be right for me to suddenly become interested in other women? I kind of feel like she's flirting with me, and I'm flirting back.

My thoughts ping-ponged back and forth like that for a few minutes, but I still couldn't come to any conclusions. All I knew for sure is that deep down in my heart I still felt guilty. But a funny thing happened minutes later when the raven-haired beauty walked back towards me with my fish dinner on a platter and Rocky's meal in a brown paper bag alongside it—with the top neatly folded over. All I could see was her. She was so attractive that the guilt weighing so heavy in my mind floated out of there like right now.

"Mmmm . . . that's going to hit the spot," I said as she lowered what looked like an oversized dinner onto the table in front of me. But then I noticed something was wrong. Raising my eyes from the steamy-hot meal, I said, "But, but I didn't order fried shrimp, too."

Putting the bag behind my platter, with her eyes still on mine, she said, "Aw, nothing to it. You look awfully hungry. Dig in."

As much as I had been blown away when I'd gotten the first glimpse of this woman, it was nothing compared to the way I was now struck by her kindness.

"Well, thanks very much, that's really kind of you. But what would your boss think?"

Waving me off and chuckling she said, "Don't worry about that. I am the boss."

"Oh, really?"

"Yup, my family has owned the place for three generations. The waitress over there is my niece. It's still a family-run operation."

Pausing then, she looked at me for a moment that seemed far longer than it actually was. No, let me correct that, she wasn't looking at me, she was studying me. And while I surely welcomed her obvious interest, I felt somewhat uncomfortable at the same time. Pulling my eyes from hers, I glanced back down at the food in front of me, looked back at her and said, "Gee, I hate to trouble you. But do you have some ketchup for the fries?"

"Oh yeah. I'm sorry," she said, as if she had suddenly snapped out of an intense dream. Then she turned and walked away.

I was afraid I'd bummed her out. No man alive likes to shun the attention of an attractive woman, but to say I was unaccustomed to situations like this would be putting it mildly. Sure, since Lorna's death I had noticed women my age occasionally taking a second look at me, sometimes ladies a bit younger. But I had been so certain that this one was out of my league, and far too young to be interested in me, that I was now in a state close to shock. I didn't know what to think. The only thing on my mind as I squeezed one of the two lemon slices over the golden-brown flounder fillets was that I'd blown a platinum opportunity. And that I'd surely road blocked her interest in me. That was what I was still thinking about when she soon came back with one of those tall, red ketchup bottles in her hand. But then I started to wonder why she had her other hand behind her back, as if hiding something.

Acting all cheery again; tilting the top of the ketchup bottle towards me, as if it aiming it me, she said in a merry voice, "Here ya go! Here's your ketchup!"

Then she gave the soft plastic bottle a good hard squeeze. And I'll be damned if a stream of red stuff didn't come flying out—directly at my face.

Cringing in my seat as I shot two open palms in front of my face to protect it, I blurted out in that dead-quiet diner, "*What the heck?*" But then the silence ended.

As if on cue the waitress, the two guys who'd been sitting at the counter and the older couple in that booth near the other end of the diner started laughing hysterically. I mean they *really* cracked up. The ketchup thingy was a practical joke. The red stuff that had spurted out the bottle at me turned out to be nothing more than a long, rubbery, gooey-looking red string. And now it was just hanging limply from the bottle's thin tip.

Embarrassed as all hell, but with this huge, goofy smile smeared on my mug instead of ketchup, all I could say was, "Nice! Very, very nice!"

That was when my new, practical-joking friend pulled the real bottle of ketchup from behind her back. Handing it to me with a warm, far-more-serious smile on her face, she asked, "You wouldn't be in the mood for company would you? Things are awfully slow right now. I can sit and talk a little, if you want me to."

Chapter 10

I was more shocked about the woman's offer to sit with me than I'd been when she shot the phony ketchup. But I could tell from her smile, the look in those tantalizing cobalt-blue eyes, and the unsure inflection in her voice, that it hadn't been easy to ask me what she did. I knew in my heart that she could feel a rare connection between us, just as I did. That one question by itself, "You wouldn't be in the mood for company, would you?" had told me volumes about her.

After taking yet another glance at Rocky out in the van, I said, "Sure. That would be nice. Care for some of my flounder?"

That was it. I was right about that connection. Her smile broadened even more, she shook her head no, and slid right into the booth. With her now sitting across from me, I got an even a stranger feeling. Somehow it felt as if we had known each other for years. And what was happening seemed perfectly natural.

"My name's Sarah, Sarah Poulin."

"George McLast," I said, extending my open hand. She took it, and as our hands locked for a moment, I added, "I just embarked on the trip of my life a few days ago. My dog Rocky and I are driving across America."

"No kidding? Isn't that exciting? Where do you live?"

"Hrmph . . . Florida, I hate to say. I can't stand it down there."

"That's not good. A person can't be happy if they hate where they live. That can only erode one's spirit."

Her last sentence really impressed me, and it told me more about her as well. Swallowing a bite of the delicious flounder, I laid my fork on the table and said, "Wow . . . 'that can only erode one's spirit'—well said."

"Oh, that's nothing earth-shattering," she came back shyly, "I just like to tinker with words sometimes is all. You see, I only work here part time anymore. I spend most of my time writing novels. I've been doing it for close to twelve years."

"No kidding? That's great. Have you had much success? I mean, do you *sell* many books?"

"Well, I definitely haven't hit the New York Times Bestseller List yet. But I do have a pretty large readership here in Maine. I'm earning enough in royalties to live on."

"That's fantastic," I said, even more impressed now, "I'm a voracious reader. I'll have to pick up one of your books sometime. What do you write?"

"I like to write about different things. As long as I think whatever I'm working on will turn out to be a worthwhile story, I keep going with it. Although my publisher wishes I wasn't, I'm what I call a "genre-jumper." Out of the fourteen novels I've written so far, about half are romances with a literary edge. The rest are suspense and historical fiction, except for one about a mistreated dog that breaks away from its owners."

"You've got to be kidding me," I said in an ironic tone as I leaned back from the table a bit. "That is wild!"

"What? Kidding about what?"

Still shocked damn near out of my out of my shorts, I said in an incredulous tone, "You wrote a book about a dog breaking free?"

Then like a hitch-hiker, I jutted a thumb toward the window alongside us and said, "I just found Rocky a few mornings ago, in North Carolina. He'd broken loose from an *abusive life*."

Leaning closer to the table then, placing her elbows on its mica top while clasping her hands together, she said, "Get out! Is that strange or what? Talk about coincidental."

As I slowly ate my meal we continued our conversation. And though we spoke about the kinds of things newly acquainted people often do, there was something very unusual about our conversation. That feeling that we had known each other for years got stronger and stronger. We spoke to each other with the ease of two old friends who'd been reunited after being apart for far too long. There were no uncomfortable pauses. There was no wondering what to say next. There were no wandering eyes. Crazy as it sounds, it seemed like we'd both been waiting our entire lives for this evening. There was so much to tell, and learn, that as soon as one of us finished saying something, the other would quickly add to what was said or fire off yet another question.

We only spent maybe twenty-five minutes together, but we covered quite a bit of ground. One of the things she told me about was her French Canadian ancestors and how they had migrated from Quebec six generations earlier. She also mentioned that most of her relatives still resided in Down East Maine, including her two, grown daughters.

After I told her a little more about the trip I was on, and how I was retracing part of John Steinbeck's route, it turned out she also knew quite a bit about his journey. When I told her I was on my way to nearby Deer Isle, and how I had been intrigued by the way Steinbeck described the place in his book, she reacted in a way I certainly didn't expect.

"He made the place sound so mysterious, so surreal," I said. "And the residents, well, he made them sound like secretive, maybe even magical people."

Hearing that, Sarah tossed her head back, stretched her farm-girl-clear eyes wide open, rolled them toward the ceiling and let out a hearty, "*Ha!*" And looking back at me she said, "You're talking about pages forty-one and forty-two in *Travels with Charley*. Well, guess what *Mister* McLast. You just happen to be looking at one of those secretive, magical people. *I live* in Deer Isle. Always have. I'm sure you know it's just fifteen minutes from here, right?"

Now I was beyond blown away. She knew the exact pages. This woman amazed me, but that didn't stop me from feeling like an utter ass. Not knowing what else to do; trying to somehow save face, I sheepishly said, "Sure, I knew I was getting close to it. But I didn't, er, I . . . ."

"Aw, I'm just kidding, silly," she waved me off, bailing me out of the tight spot I'd put myself in.

The longer we talked the more I wanted to find out more about Sarah Poulin. And she wasn't keeping it a secret that she wanted to know more about me. Of course, she didn't say that but I could tell. Human intuition can at times be an amazingly perceptive sense. And I was sure mine was at the top of its game.

Sitting there, getting to know her, I was no longer sixty-six years old. I felt like I was in my twenties again. There were no heart troubles casting dark shadows inside my mind. The dread of eventually having to go back to Florida was nonexistent. The fact that I didn't have much money, that my financial security was as wobbly as it was, didn't matter either. Nothing bothered me. I was liberated from my worries and problems and felt hopeful. For the time being at least I didn't even worry about what Lorna might have thought about me showing an interest in another woman. No, the way this intelligent woman with the slight Maine accent and full-of-life candid personality studied my eyes when I spoke, that pulled just about every ounce of negativity out of my head. But there was one thing lingering in a corner of my mind that did still concern me. I wondered if she had any idea how old I actually was. As I said earlier a lot of people mistook me to be considerably younger than I actually was. And if this encounter kept going as well as it had been, I knew I'd have no choice but to be honest with her.

The only times Sarah pulled her eyes from mine for a second or two during our conversation was when more customers came into the diner or when glancing at her niece to be sure she was handling everything okay. The last time she looked away was when I had just finished eating and was blotting my mouth with a napkin, as a family of five walked in through the entrance.

"That really hit the spot," I said, placing the napkin on my empty plate, "but I suppose I'd better get rolling now. It looks like your niece is getting awfully busy. And Rocky must be famished out there."

"Yup," she said, looking a little downcast for the first time, "I think she needs a helping hand."

I picked up the check and put my palms on the table to get up. But I wasn't going anywhere yet. My hostess leaned across the mica top and placed *her hand* atop one of mine. Freezing in the position I was in, feeling the blood rush to my head, I wondered, *what is this all about?*

"George," she said with her face still dead serious, "you said you planned on staying in Deer Isle for a day or two. Where are you going to camp? Have you reserved a site at a campground?"

"Well . . . no. Not yet. I saw in my directory that there's a campground about five miles back from where I just came from. And there's another one the other way, beyond Deer Isle, in Stonington. So I thought I'd . . . ."

"Look," she said, giving my hand a gentle squeeze, "I know this is kind of a, well, an odd situation. And sure, we've only just met, but I feel . . . I feel like I know you really well. What do you say you camp out at my place? There's plenty of room. I have ten acres. Not only that, but I'm off tomorrow. And I can get somebody to cover the next day for me."

With a hint of that smile then finding its way back on her face, she added, "Nobody knows this area any better than I do. What do you say? I can show you and Rocky around some?"

I glanced down at her hand *still* on top of mine and looked back at her. With my mind debating whether or not it would be *right* to accept her offer, my eyes narrowed and I bit down lightly on the side of my lower lip. I did not want to say what I was about to, but I knew I had no choice.

"Listen . . . Sarah," I said in a low voice, "I don't know where any of this might possibly lead, but I have to be honest with you. You might not realize it, but I'm in my mid-sixties." Then slowly turning my head from side to side, I continued, "I have a son who is forty. You, you can't be much older than that. I hate to say it but I don't think you want to . . . ."

"Well aren't you the sweetest man to ever come down the pike?" she interrupted while slowly sliding her hand off mine. "I'll let you in on a little secret, if you promise not to tell anybody while you're here."

"Sure, scout's honor."

She glanced around one time, looked back at me, and in a low voice said, "It just so happens I'll be *fifty* this coming Saturday."

"Get out of here!"

The only visible signs that she could be nearing anywhere close to that age were the few barely-discernible, hair-thin lines alongside the outside corners of her eyes. Had I not left my reading glasses on after perusing the menu earlier I never would have noticed.

"Really, I kid you not. You know how we short people are. We often belie our years."

Without saying another thing she reached across the table, pulled the check from my hand, and with her niece's yellow pencil started jotting something on the back side of it. I know this may sound stupid, but with her head down as she wrote, I thought how the part on top of her head was probably the neatest, straightest one I'd ever seen.

"Here ya go," she said a moment later, handing me the check. "Here's my address and some short directions." And with a hopeful look on her face, she added, "George, I'd really, really enjoy showing you around a bit. And like I said, I've got plenty of room at my place. We could even run an extension cord from the house to your van, so you'd have electricity. Come on. What do you say? Don't be a poop."

What the hell, I thought, *I'm on the adventure of a lifetime, right? Why not? I'd be crazy to pass up this chance. I could have a nice time for a couple of days and resume the trip after that.*

"Heck yes!" I said, "Why not? But you're sure I won't be putting you out, right?"

She slid out of the booth, stood over me, and rested a hand on my shoulder. "Take those chicken tenders out to Rocky now. Go to my place, park anywhere you like, and make yourself at home. I'll be there in a little over an hour."

She gave me a little wink and was just about to turn around and head back to the counter when I shook my head no, saying, "Whoa, hold on a minute. Let me pay you for the . . . ."

All she said was, "Goodbye, George. See you in a little while," and walked away.

As I made my way out of the diner, my head was a cyclone of whirling, exciting thoughts. But it didn't stay that way very long. The instant I stepped out the doorway, all that good stuff was gone. As if my brain had been on a speeding, out-of-control merry-go-round and the operator slammed it to a stop, my thoughts returned to the real world. And the nanosecond it did, that deep, undeniable, all-knowing voice inside my head gave me hell.

What are you doing, man? Sure, she's gorgeous, smart and all that, but you can't get involved at this point in your life. Face it! You're over the hill and ill. Not only that but you're on the trip you dreamed about for years—the trip you and Lorna dreamed about. Yeah, that's right, Lorna. What about her? You know this just isn't right, none of it. Sorry my friend, but you need to do an about face, march your ass back in there, and tell her thanks but no thanks.

Chapter 11

As I stood atop the diner's steps in deep thought, the Maine sun was no longer in sight. It had fallen beneath the horizon and dusk was setting in. Downright nippy out by now, and that voice in my head was still telling me to go back inside—call this off—go on with my trip and my life. Turning around after that, I put my hand on the cool, metal door handle. But something happened just as I was about to push it open. Through the glass I saw Sarah Poulin's face again. She was placing short stout glasses of water in front of the five family members who'd entered the diner minutes earlier. And her lovely face was all lit up with that warm smile of hers.

"Screw it." I told myself.

With the directions and paper bag still in hand, I turned and climbed down the red brick steps. And as I did I drowned out that inner voice with a train of thoughts.

This might not go anywhere, and it probably won't, but I'm not going to blow this chance. For God's sake, nobody's saying I'm going to run off and get married. There's nothing wrong with having a little company for a day or two. I'm sure there'll be times on the road when I'll be starving for some. That's it! I'm going!

Rocky nearly went berserk when I unlocked the van door. The little bugger had been watching me like a hawk since I'd come out of Poulin's Down East Diner. When I got in and sat behind the wheel, he was all over me like right now. I don't know what was moving faster, his tiny pink tongue licking my face or that stubby tail. After stroking his head a few times, I broke out the goodies and boy, did he ever dig into those chicken bits. I fed him one piece at a time, but he barely chewed them. He just about inhaled them. Once he had finished I wiped my fingertips with the napkin Sarah had put in the bag, took a look at the directions on the check, and headed for the Deer Isle Bridge.

After driving a few miles through a canyon of tall evergreen trees that appeared gray in the dissipating light, I spotted the old iron bridge. The quiet road I'd been on had led me up to the top of a hill, and as I now peered down and off into the distance, it was an incredible sight—breathtaking but eerie at the same time.

The steel suspension bridge, with its two towering pedestals that seemed to reach the sky, looked to be a subtle blue-green—a color that put me to mind of copper that had oxidized for too many years in rough weather. The nearly deserted, two-lane structure rose in the center forming a hump way high above a slate-gray arm of the Atlantic. What added to the vision's spookiness, though, was the low fog lifting from the dark water. It seemed as if the dead-calm water was boiling hot, yet I knew that this far north it had to be plenty cold. Out near the far end of the bridge, I spotted a small islet that looked to be solid granite. But somehow a lone scraggly pine tree had managed to grow. As for Deer Isle itself, from where I was on the opposite side of the bridge, it looked like an uninhabited, densely-forested island. About all I could see were tree tops. Still descending that hill in the last remnants of daylight like I was, I knew that the panoramic view before me was one I'd be able to pull up in my mind for as long as I might live. It was that surreal. However, when Rocky and I motored across the bridge moments later, I felt like I was driving into a dream—a dreamlike Mecca of total peacefulness.

By now it become downright cold for September. I cranked my window all the way closed and picked the check up from the console. Alternating glances at the neatly written directions and what lie ahead in the beams of my headlights, I saw that I was only three quick turns from the road Sarah lived on. I also saw on the gracefully written directions that her address was number 1 Poulin Lane.

Hmmm, she said that her family had been here for generations. She obviously wasn't kidding.

A few short minutes later, after driving slowly through a dense forest of spruce trees, I saw a sign on the side of the road. It read Poulin Lane and I made a right turn. I idled slowly through about another hundred yards of dark forest before a house appeared in my high beams. A stone structure two stories high, it looked like something out of a fairy tale.

"We're here, Rocky," I said, giving his head a little massage. He'd been lying motionless next to me and still didn't move a muscle. "Yeah, pal, I'm tired, too. It's been a long day. We were in Maryland this morning now we're all the way up here in Maine."

I pulled into the driveway, rolled about halfway to the garage on the left side of the house, and steered onto the grass alongside it.

"I guess this is as good a place as any," I said, coming to a stop.

After killing the lights and engine I let go of the wheel. Tired as I was, I just dropped my hands onto my lap and let my head flop back against the headrest. As I looked up at the van's headliner in the darkness, all I could say was, "Whoosh! Am I ever *exhausted*?" Then my mind went to work, and I again started beating myself up.

I hope I didn't make a mistake coming here. Do I have a right to be here? I spent almost my entire adult life with Lorna. Even if nothing becomes of this, am I doing the right thing, trying to push her from my mind, and coming here? Shit man, I don't need this. I can't put myself through the wringer right now. I don't have the energy. And for crying out loud I'm only going to spend a night here, two at the most. I'll just let her show me around the peninsula tomorrow. After that I can get back on the road or leave early the next morning. That's what I'll do. That's the end of it.

I reached for the pack of cigarettes standing in one of the console drink holders, lit one up, and rolled the window down a crack. After taking a hit I looked out through the windshield. Although there were all kinds of splattered bugs on the glass and full darkness had set in, I could see a sliver of moon straight in front of me. Directly beneath it I saw something else—it's reflection.

Wow! She must be on the water here.

Turning toward Rocky then I snapped the new leash onto his harness saying, "Come on, buddy, let's go for a little walk." That perked him up real quick. Although he was still half asleep, he jumped right up on all fours. I scooped him up from the seat, lowered him onto the grass outside the van, and closed the door. As soon as I did, I heard a dog start barking somewhere inside the stone house. And I realized there wasn't just one, there were two. From the sound of their barks they were pretty good-sized dogs, too.

As we strolled past the back of the house toward the water a moment later, the robust barks no longer sounded so loud, and I heard the emphatic call of a whip-poor-will in the forest off to the left. Knowing that the rarely-seen species was mostly heard in the summer months, I immediately thought it odd to be hearing the classic call so late in the year. But I didn't dwell on the sound very long.

Just a few steps later, when Rocky stopped to do his business, I was suddenly awestruck. In the moon's dim light I saw that a long stretch of calm, seemingly black, water a short distance in front us. It started at the end of the backyard and continued straight out for what looked to be about a mile. Maybe a quarter mile wide and devoid of any piers or docks, I'd still call it a harbor. And was it ever impressive? In the moonlight it was the kind of vision that famed Maine painter Winslow Homer could have done wonders with, had he been sitting behind his easel where I stood. Like most of what I'd seen of Deer Isle, the shores on both sides of the water were lined with tall spruce trees—packed so close together one would wonder how the isle's namesake deer could even fit between them. There were only two lights visible out there—one on each side of the harbor. And since the dim glows were both back in the woods instead of out on the water, I assumed they were from houses. Along both shorelines I could just make out a scattering of huge rocks that seemed to be standing sentinel in the darkness.

Making my way near the water's edge then I thought, *Talk about paradise! This place is nothing short of amazing. I'll bet that, other than those two lights off in the distance, this harbor looks just as it did a thousand years ago. I can't wait to see what it looks like when the sun comes up tomorrow.*

I knelt down on one knee next to Rocky then and raised my eyes toward the sky. Stroking his furry back, I said in voice graced with more wonderment than it had had in ages, "Look up there Rockster. Have you ever seen so many stars? I swear this vision would give old Vincent's Starry Starry Night a run for its money. The sky looks as if ten-thousand luminous, sparkling-white grains of sand had been thrown up there and they stuck."

After surveying the scene a little while longer, we headed back across the wide, grassy yard toward the van. With the leash's looped end in one hand and the filter of my stubbed-out cigarette in the other, I thought how I could easily get to love a place like this. But I didn't entertain that thought very long. For just as I opened the driver's side door of the van, two beams of light appeared up the road—lighting up Rocky and I like two stunned deer in headlights. And that's exactly what they were—headlights. Quickly realizing it must be Sarah returning home, I leaned into the van and across the front seat, pulled out the dashboard ashtray, put the cigarette butt in it and slid it closed again. Then what looked like a Subaru Forester pulled alongside us. In the darkness I couldn't tell exactly what color it was, but those dogs inside the house certainly knew who was driving it. They were barking to beat the band.

The second Sarah came to a stop I became a bundle of nerves. Standing there in the darkness after she killed the lights and shut off the engine, I felt excited, nervous, and uncomfortable, all at the same time. But it dawned on me that she had gotten home much faster than she said she would, and I knew that was no accident. I knew she must have been so anxious to see me again that she somehow finagled her way out of the diner earlier than planned. I felt hugely flattered, but unlike back at the diner, I now didn't know what to say to her. And again I hated myself for feeling like an awkward, infatuated teenager. But this time I felt something else as well. It was my heart. It had been doing better since I'd left Florida—only flipping two or three times a day. And each time that squeezing feeling had been feint. But it was different now. As I watched Sarah get out of her SUV, the life-sustaining muscle inside my chest stuttered not once, not twice, but three consecutive times. They were long pauses, too. And each time that life-sustaining muscle kicked back over, it thumped harder than it ever had before. So hard it felt like a fist jabbing at the inside of my rib cage.

Oh shit! What's happening here? I don't need this now. This can't be the end. Not now. Not here.

Cold as it was, my palms had become sweaty and I suddenly felt claustrophobic. I felt like the forest, the water in back, the house, that starry sky, all of it was closing in on me. And as Sarah walked towards me I felt the same way about her.

Oh no! No, no, no, no, no. This is not good. Why does this have to happen now?

Chapter 12

"Well," Sarah said, as she rounded the back of the SUV and approached me and Rocky. "It looks like you boys found the place okay."

Somehow, as if they were magical, the jovial tone of her voice and the smile on her face instantly calmed me down. That quickly, the herky-jerky beat of my faulty heart smoothed out. That paralyzing end-of-the-world feeling of grave dread that had overwhelmed me disintegrated into the nighttime air. I was still a little shaken, but it wasn't enough to stop me from feeling excited to be with this woman again.

"Yeah, Sarah," I said, her name feeling so very special when it left my mouth, "with your directions it was a snap. I hope you don't mind but we took a little stroll in your backyard. And wow, I can't wait to see what that harbor looks like in the daylight tomorrow. I'll bet the view's to die for."

"You know, George," she answered, taking a glance back there in the darkness, "some people have more money than God. They can own a sprawling oceanfront home in Florida, a highfalutin ranch in the Colorado Rockies, or both. But after a while most of them get used to it. They look out their windows and often don't even notice the beauty. It's human nature. And I really believe that's the way it is with a lot of people. But the view back *here*, and I'm not just saying this because it's mine, I've never taken it for granted. You'll see what I mean in the morning. It's . . . it's an almost-spiritual vision."

Leaning comfortably against the back of my van with my arms crossed by now, I said, "I'm sure you're right. Dark as it is right now, it's still super impressive."

For the next few moments neither of us said a word. Everything had become quiet. Sarah's dogs had stopped barking, and with not a breath of wind rustling the pines, it was as if the world had come to a stop. But then she smiled at me. It was a warm, tender smile. As I stood there looking down at her, at the reflection of the moon in her eyes, I smiled back at her. For as long as our eyes locked, you would think such an affectionate exchange among near strangers would have become awkward. But it didn't. We held our gazes just a little longer before she glanced across the front yard and looked back at me.

"Listen George McLast, it's kind of nippy out here tonight. Why don't you and Rocky—you weary travelers, come inside tonight? I . . . I've got three spare bedrooms. You both can get a good night's sleep, and it'll be warm."

This caught me off guard. Not knowing what else to say, I unraveled my crossed arms and shoved my hands deep into the front pockets of my jeans before answering her.

"Oh, I couldn't do that, Sarah. Thanks so much. But we, we'll be fine in the van. I don't know how Rocky might react to your dogs or how they would to him. So far he doesn't seem to get along all that well with other animals." Then, tilting my head a bit to the side, referring to the van behind me, I added, "I have a new portable heater in there, and knowing we might get into some really cold weather during our trip, tonight would be a good night to try it out. It's kind of cool but not that bad."

Talk about feeling lousy. As if I had blindsided Sarah with a sucker punch, her smile shrunk some. I could see she was fighting to keep what was left of it but that didn't make me feel one ounce better. I said what I did because I knew I'd be very uncomfortable sleeping in another woman's home after being married to Lorna for so many years. Not only that, but what Lorna might have thought about me doing such a thing was also part of the reason I told Sarah no. But none of that had made it easy. And seeing the undeniable disappointment now on her sweet face made me want to hop into the van and peel out of there. But I couldn't.

What I did next may sound like I was jumping the gun. It might seem a bit premature considering the short time we'd known one another. But I couldn't stop myself. Seeing her so looking so sad made it feel like the right thing to do, the only thing. I pulled my back from where I was resting on the van, took a step closer to her and I gently put my hand on her shoulder. And I held it as I spoke—punctuating my words with tender, caring squeezes.

With my eyebrows arched, I moved my head from side to side slowly and said, "I can't let this go just like that. I have to be totally honest with you because it's my nature. You see, I lost my wife three years ago but it feels like just three months have passed. It was the shock of my life. She died . . . well, let's just say unexpectedly. We'd been married for forty-one years. She was the only woman I ever loved, Sarah." With my eyes damp and misty by now, I paused a second or two before adding, "I hope you'll understand."

Her face was dead serious now, but her voice was full of heartfelt sympathy when she laid her small hands softly on my chest and said, "You bet, George. Of course, I understand."

With our eyes embraced in an emotional embrace, we stood there for a long moment saying nothing. Words were no longer necessary. Our eyes did our talking. I was without a doubt sure that she felt the exact same way as I did. I knew she, too, was thinking, where on earth have you been all this time? What's kept us apart? We were made for each other. We were destined to be together.

But then something else drifted into it my mind. My damned subconscious shoved its way into this tender moment. It demanded that I back off some. It told me I was getting too close to this woman; that I had health problems, mourning issues, and that I couldn't let anything step in the way of my cross-country trip. It told me the journey was going to be my last hurrah—that odds were I wouldn't be around much longer, and I had no right getting Sarah's hopes up for anything different. It isn't fair, my thought center barked at me, forget about it. Just thank her now, spend the night, and split in the morning—early in the morning.

I hated that damn all-knowing voice.

Screw all that, I thought as I still looked into those compassionate eyes, *I'm not paying heed to anything you say. Not now, anyway. Not at this moment. Go get yourself lost!*

It was then that Sarah spoke again, still softly and slowly.

"I can't say I can empathize with you, because . . . because I've never lost somebody I loved dearly. All I can do is imagine the hurt you must feel. I've never experienced it. Sure, I lost a husband I once loved. But by the time he left me, almost all that love was gone. All I had left were memories of how it once had been, and they were faded, obsolete."

Removing her fingertips from my chest, trying to look and sound upbeat, she said, "Listen, you and Rocky get all the rest you need out here tonight. I'll see you in the morning. Are you an early riser?"

"Yeah, Sarah, I'm an early riser." I said, and doing my part to try to lighten the moment I finished with, "Early to bed early to rise, right?"

"You betcha, I'm the same way. And first thing tomorrow I'm going to make you guys a really special breakfast. How's that sound?"

"That'd be terrific. It's been a while since I've had a good home-cooked breakfast."

"Oh," she came back with an impish look, "I was thinking raisin bran."

Thinking she was kidding but not totally sure, I shrugged my shoulders. "Sure . . . sure, raisin bran will work."

She grinned so wide that her face seemed to light up the darkness. And giving me a playful slap on the chest, she said, "Go to sleep, George. I'll see you in the AM."

After Sarah stepped inside her house, I took the two Adirondack chairs out of the back of the van. Then I hoisted Rocky and myself inside, closed the doors, slid the curtains closed, and hooked my new/reconditioned, sixty-nine-dollar Cabela's heater up to my propane tank. That was all she wrote. I pulled the comforter over myself and my partner. Seven-thirty or no seven-thirty we were unconscious in a matter of minutes. And did we ever sleep. We were out like two bears in mid-winter hibernation. You could have prodded us with a log poker and we wouldn't have felt a thing. Yes, we were that tired, comfortable, and toasty. The last thing I remember before falling off was the calm, content feeling that warmed me inside.

Chapter 13

The next morning Rocky woke me up. Lying beside me beneath my arm, he started to growl. They were low, long growls and I wondered what on earth could be bothering him. Did he suddenly not like the feel of my arm on him? Thinking that that might be the reason made me feel very uneasy. Was there a side of him I hadn't yet noticed?

With the blue curtains dimly lit by the rising sun outside I removed my arm, rolled over and picked up my watch. The digital numbers read 6:31, and Rocky was growling more fervently.

"What's wrong?" I asked him, even more concerned by now. "What's with you this morning?"

As if that last question had set him off he jerked his body up on all fours, leapt clear over me, and standing on his hind legs, started scratching at the curtains maniacally. He wanted to kill whatever was behind them.

"For crying out loud calm down, will you?" I said pushing myself up a bit with one arm. "What is it?"

Pushing the curtain to the side, I could see what was driving him batty. Only about forty feet from our eyes there were moose—two of them, and they were huge. One was a female and the other had a rack of broad antlers wider than I could stretch my arms.

"Oh, it's okay, Rocky," I whispered while sliding my hand down the standing fur on his back, "they're just nibbling on the grass out there. Hey, look at the antlers on the bigger one. They're velvety covering is all ragged. And it's peeling off because it's rutting season. We certainly don't want to get him aggravated."

Rocky did calm down considerably after hearing my unruffled soothing voice, but he wouldn't stop that low growling. He kept it up for roughly ten minutes, until the two largest members of the deer family slowly made their way back into the tree line and we lost sight of them. I could not believe how lucky I was to have seen them on my very first morning in Maine. Feeling both rested and excited now, I was as happy as a kid on the first day of summer vacation. Lickety-split I got out of my long-woolen underwear and put on a clean sweatshirt and jeans. I felt so alive that even the two consecutive thumps my heart did when I was pulling on my high-top sneakers did nothing to damper my mood.

Once I was completely dressed, I combed my hair and stuffed my wallet and keys into my pockets. Then I clicked the heater off, snapped the leash onto Rocky's harness and took him outside. But before I even closed the doors behind me, I realized it was really cold. Knowing the blue sweatshirt I had on wasn't going to cut it, I grabbed my hooded black one and pulled it on, too.

Just as I'd seen coming from the nostrils of the two moose, misty streams of vapor pushed out of mine every time I exhaled. It was that cold this late September morning. But the air was still, and after all the stifling hot months I'd spent in Florida I relished it. With plenty of bounce in our steps, Rocky and I then strolled toward the water in back. And wow, what a view it was in the early morning light. I could now see why Sarah had said the night before that she never tired of it. The jagged, rocky shorelines on both sides of the harbor—the green, conical pines mixed with a scattering of red and gold deciduous trees—the long stretch of mysterious dark water framed by them—all of it beneath a clear blue sky made for one unforgettable sight. The new day's sun sitting like a bright floating sphere atop the watery horizon certainly didn't detract from it, either.

As I stood at the water's edge, with the sun's reflection stretching the entire length of the harbor like a glowing pink trail all the way to my feet, I heard a window open.

"Good morning, boys!" A merry voice chirped from behind me. "Are you hungry yet?"

Turning around with that mist now streaming from my mouth, I answered, "You bet we are. But I don't know if I should bring Rocky in with your dogs, Sarah."

"Oh, I think they'll be just fine. The door back here's open. Take your time and come in whenever you're ready."

"Sounds like a plan. We'll be in just a few minutes."

As we poked around the sprawling yard a wee bit longer, I heard a resounding knock-knock-knock sound coming from a nearby tree. A large pileated woodpecker was hunting for its breakfast two-thirds up the trunk. Then two black-capped chickadees flew side by side out of the forest, and I remembered reading somewhere that they were Maine's state bird. But that's when my bird watching ended. Rocky lifted his nose up high and was doing some serious sniffing. I too picked up the scent. Sarah had left the kitchen window open a crack, and the delicious aroma of hot, grilling pancakes wafted from it.

To my surprise Rocky behaved like a perfect gentleman when we inside the house. My hostesses two golden retrievers—Lewis and Clark, were very low-key and that certainly helped. They just sniffed Rocky a little and he did the same to them. Once we were sure that they were okay, Sarah put three bowls of dog food in a corner of the country kitchen and they all went to town. As for those pancakes, they were scrumptious. Chock full of fresh blueberries a friend had given Sarah; we smeared bits of margarine on top of them and poured on some steamy-hot, pure maple syrup. Not only was the breakfast out of this world, but Sarah and I both felt like old friends as we spoke. I felt bad when telling her I'd have to pass on the sausages she'd cooked, but she fully understood. And when my heart skipped a couple of times as we ate, I, of course, said nothing. No matter where our relationship might possibly be heading, my malfunctioning heart wasn't something I was ready to share.

By the time I was adding a bit of cream to my second cup of coffee, I said, "Sarah, if you don't mind, I'm going to step out onto the back deck to smoke a cigarette."

For a short moment she looked at me with a surprised expression on her face. But that certainly didn't come as a shocker. Not after the way the twenty-first century media had engraved in the minds of the American public that anybody who smoked a cigarette was a bottom-level lowlife, and in all probability a person of questionable morals. It was because of that nonsense that I had in the past actually severed a few relationships. I'd also courteously refused invitations to people's homes when I felt it might be a problem. My mind had long been made up. Anybody who didn't like my smoking could go directly to hell. I was who I was. I'd been smoking for close to fifty years, albeit lightly for most of that time, and I wasn't going to change for anybody who had bought into that bad guy/loser myth. Still, I was about to explain to Sarah how an after-a-meal smoke, to me, was like a Pavlovian reaction. But I didn't. I didn't have to go that far.

"My father smokes cigars," she said, "and I would never send him out on the deck to do it. You stay right where you are and I'll get you the ashtray I reserve for him."

Of course, I was glad to hear that.

"Thanks much," I said after she'd taken the clean ashtray out of a knotty pine cabinet and laid it down on the table next to me.

Then, sounding like an excited kid, she said, "I've got big plans for us today. How would you like to go up to Bar Harbor and Acadia National Park? I know I told you I'd show you around Deer Isle, but we can do that pretty quickly and then head north. Acadia's only a little over an hour north of here."

Since I'd been driving for four days, I preferred to stay around Deer Isle, but without as much as a flinch, I said, "Sure. We can do that. I really should see the park while I'm up here."

"Terrific! We'll take my SUV and I'll drive. You're probably ready for a little R and R after coming all the way up from Florida."

"Are you sure you don't mind? I can . . . ."

"No way, George," she shook her head. "You're my guest and I'm the tour director. I'm going to do the driving." Then rising to her feet and picking up our empty plates, she added, "Just let me straighten up here for a few minutes, and we'll get a nice early start. It's going to be a gorgeous day."

And it was a gorgeous day. After driving around Deer Isle we headed north through the small towns of Brooksville, Blue Hill, and Surry. Most of the scenery between them was rural and absolutely breathtaking. With rolling hills, nearly deserted curvy roads cutting through dense forests, a scattering of pastures, and only a house here and there beneath the clear blue autumn sky, I told Sarah I could very easily call such an area home. When I added that I wouldn't care how much snow came down in the winter months, I realized my raving about the place might not have been a good idea. Because she had turned her eyes from the road to me and they looked very hopeful.

Yes, I know that sounds ludicrous considering we hadn't even known each other for twenty-four hours yet. But I'd seen that hope. And why else would she have turned to me after I said what I had? Whether the vibes I'd gotten were right on target or dead wrong, I quickly turned around to Rocky in the back seat and asked him if he was enjoying himself. I didn't know what else I could do to dispel my uneasiness. I was only going to spend this one day with Sarah Poulin and that was going to be it. The following morning, come hell or high water, my furry copilot and I would hit the road again.

Despite all that, we had one heck of a good time on Mount Desert Island, though it didn't start out well. When we rolled up to the entrance at Acadia National Park, I insisted on paying the entrance fee. But I was not happy when I found out the cost of it. Down in Florida I had gotten an "America the Beautiful" senior pass for free entry. into National Parks and National Wildlife Areas, but as it turned out Acadia is one of the few parks in the country that didn't accept them. And when the attendant told us the fee to get in was *twenty-five dollars,* I had to fight hard not to go ballistic. Then it got worse. She said the fee was good for seven days and that made me angrier yet. I knew that I, and many more visitors like me, were being taken advantage by the U.S. National Park Service. The so-called *service* knew better than anyone that the huge majority of visitors to Acadia were day trippers, but yet they didn't offer a single-day entry fee. Since Sarah was sitting right beside me, and the stout woman with the Down

East accent who took my money had nothing to do with making park policies, I didn't make an all-out scene over the rip off. But when I forked over twenty-five smackers, I certainly wasn't going to smile about it either.

Despite the fee fiasco, we did have a great day. The sprawling, rugged scenery in the park was like nothing I'd ever seen before. The twisting road to the top of Cadillac Mountain afforded us incredible views—memorable vistas I would not soon forget. But driving up the mountainside is not for the weak hearted. Many areas along the narrow, snaking road had no guardrails. Some did have widely-spaced rows of large rocks, but it still seemed like we were motoring up the very edge of the earth. Granted, by mountain standards Cadillac isn't considered huge. But when you're looking almost straight down, out of a vehicle's passenger seat like I was, fifteen-hundred feet is a long, long way. And when you look out into the distance, the view you see is one to die for. It's as if you can see all the way to the opposite end of the planet. There's nothing but forests, old rolling mountains, rocky shorelines, lakes, bays, and ocean. Being we were up there in autumn didn't hurt either. With the air crisp and clear as it was, and all the green, yellow, and fire-red trees in the distance looking electrified, the entire vision seemed three dimensional.

Once we reached the parking area near the top of the mountain, the three of us climbed steep slabs of granite to the summit. And as we peered down we could see the quaint town of Bar Harbor and even more ocean beyond it.

"Wow, Sarah," I said, as a brisk cool breeze lifted my hair from my forehead, "this park *is* something else."

"Yes, it sure is," she said with her eyes still trained down on Bar Harbor. "I've been coming here all my life, yet every time I come back I'm still mesmerized by all this beauty. It has a very similar effect on me just as my view at home does."

"I can see why. This is one beautiful state, and I envy you for being fortunate enough to live in a place you love so much."

"That's right," she said, lifting her gaze from the town below and looking into my eyes with a concerned look on her face, "you mentioned something about not liking Florida last night."

"Yeah, I did. But you know what? I don't want to even think about that place now. I'm just so glad to be away from it. If I ever make it back . . . ." I caught myself then. Stopping what I was saying mid-sentence, I felt like kicking myself for almost spilling the beans about my health problem. Instead, though, I quickly I rephrased what I was saying.

"What I mean is, even if I somehow find a way not to have to live in Florida again, I'd still have to go back there after my trip. You know, to tie up loose ends and all that."

I didn't like the way she was now looking at me atop that mountain. It was as if she was once again reading my thoughts. No, she couldn't have had a clue that I had a heart problem, but there was a questioning look in her penetrating, blue eyes.

"Hey," I said, forcing a more jovial tone into my voice, "where are we going next? This is your neck of the woods and you're the tour guide."

That suspicious look lingered for a short moment, but as soon as it began to fade, Sarah pointed down at the village. "See that little blue speck down there, the sky-blue one on the right side of town?"

"Yeah, I see it. It's a rooftop."

"Exactly, it's the roof of a great little restaurant. A close friend I grew up with owns it. She and I have had an unmentioned understanding for years—I never charge her when she comes to eat at the diner, and she never charges me when I go to her place. What do you say? Want to go there for lunch later? The food is wicked good, and they have tables set up outside on the patio this time of the year. I wanted to take you into town anyway."

"The food is *wicked good*?" I said, exaggeratedly lifting my eyebrows way up near my hairline, "Why is it I'm seeing an evil green witch standing in front of a steaming hot cauldron when you say that?"

"Oh silly," Sarah came back, playfully slapping me on the shoulder. "Wicked good is just a Maine thing. It means that something is really, really good."

"Well then, I'm definitely game for that. But there's a bit of a problem." I looked down at Rocky. "We'll have to be able to find a place to park close to the restaurant. I might be a little overprotective, but I'd have to keep an eye on the Rockster, here. I just feel a lot more comfortable leaving him alone if I'm able to watch him."

"Not a problem. The patio at Loretta's place is dog friendly."

"Really? Well that sounds like a winner. Let's do it. Hopefully he'll behave like a gentleman."

"Oh he'll be fine, won't you Rocky?" she said, bending over, giving him a little scratch behind both his ears.

Shortly after that we drove back down the mountain, and Sarah showed me some more places in Acadia. On the seashore side of the park, we got out and walked to Thunder Hole where, when conditions are right, you can hear a resounding boom as water breaks into the rock formation. We also parked at

Eagle Lake and walked along one of the Carriage Roads that John D. Rockefeller had built many years earlier. With the autumn air so crisp and invigorating, and all the foliage bursting with color all around us, I knew I was taking a stroll I wouldn't soon forget. Of course, having Sarah Poulin at my side had something to do with it as well.

After we had left the park and were heading toward the restaurant, Sarah gave me some strict orders. She told me not to order lobster at her friend's place, because on the way home she wanted to buy two at an Ellsworth lobster pound and cook them up for dinner. So when we got to Loretta's Lobster Etcetera, we both ordered Portobello Mushroom sandwiches on fresh-baked focaccia bread. And let me tell you, with hot melted Monterey Jack cheese on them, they were out of this world. Sarah's friend turned out to be a winner, too. Loretta Michaud was a warm, friendly, down-home lady who could not do enough for us. A vivacious Mainer, she not only insisted that we had a bowl of clam chowder with our sandwiches but she also brought out a nice piece of roasted chicken for Rocky.

All in all it was a fabulous day. And dinner that night was no letdown either. I was treated to what had to be the best lobster to ever come out of the North Atlantic. Not only that, but Sarah made some unbelievable crab cake hushpuppies as well. Good as everything was though, and despite what they say about the way to a man's heart being through his stomach, this woman could have fed me cold Spam and she still would have made it just as deep into my ailing heart. Yes, I had fallen head over heels for her. And nothing was going to change that. Even the visions of Lorna that had drifted into my mind from time to time throughout that day couldn't prevent it. For the first time since her death, I started thinking there just might not be anything wrong with trying to make what was left of my life a better experience. But shortly after dinner all my positive feelings and optimism deserted me. As Sarah and I walked Rocky outside in the darkness, my outlook suddenly darkened as well. I glanced at my van alongside the stone house it was a stark reminder that I'd be leaving in the morning.

Struggling to maintain the same upbeat tone that had been in my voice all day, I said, "It's another nice night," as we looked out at the harbor and strolled toward it.

"Yes, it sure is," Sarah said. But now her voice was by no means cheery, and I knew why. She was thinking about the same thing I was. But I waited. Neither of us said a thing until we stopped at the water's edge, turned to me, and in the same unsettled tone said, "I don't want to be pushy, George. If your mind is made up, I'll understand. But . . . but I'd sure love it if you could stay a few more days. There's so much more I want to show . . . ."

I interrupted her right there. I'd heard enough. Although I had already made up my mind that I wasn't going to string her along, my heart somehow commandeered my tongue. I found myself saying, "I'll tell you what. Your birthday's on Saturday, right?"

"Yes, Saturday," she answered, with new hope returning those captivating eyes of hers.

"Okay, I'll tell you what. If it's not too much trouble, Rocky and I'll stay until Sunday morning. But Sarah, I really have to get going then."

Some of that hope vanished. And I knew she was struggling to keep her smile intact when, still looking up at me, she said in a tone that approached solemn, "I'll settle for that, for now, anyway."

126

For the next three days the weather remained perfect and we again had some terrific times. Among other places, Sarah took me and Rocky to the quaint seaside town of Stonington. We also went to the nearby Good Life Center at Forest Farm where the late Scott and Helen Nearing had lived off the land long before the movement had its resurgence in the mid-1960s. As each day came to an end, my new friend and I became closer. Our feelings for each other grew stronger and stronger and did some homesteading of their own. Both of us had taken up residence in one another's hearts. And by the time each day came to an end, we both had claimed bigger pieces. But as the old saying goes, all good things must come to an end. At about eight-thirty Saturday night, after I'd taken her out for a nice birthday dinner in Stonington, Sarah pulled her Subaru alongside my parked van for the last time. And when we got out of the SUV in the darkness, she hadn't a clue what was coming, but I felt it was time to say goodbye.

"Want to take a stroll in back?" she asked.

"Sure, why not?"

As we ambled across the grass, noticing there wasn't a single star visible in the sky, I said, "I guess the clouds must have moved in while we were eating."

Tilting her pretty head way back, seeing the same thing I did, she said, "Yup, it feels like it's going to rain, too. I guess we've been so busy that we haven't had time to worry about weather forecasts, have we?"

Then it happened. With the end of Rocky's leash in my right hand, and him walking on that side of me, I felt something take a hold of my other hand. It was Sarah's hand.

During the few days we had been together, I'd wanted to take hers a few times. And I thought for sure she wanted to do the same thing. I knew she'd been fighting the urge just as I had. I also believed that the main reason she hadn't was because I'd told her I was still mourning Lorna. But since I knew now just how deeply Sarah cared for me and how considerate of my feelings she'd been, I wanted to stop in my tracks, slide my arms around her, and kiss her like I hadn't kissed in years. But I only did part of that. I stopped walking. And when I did she did, too. My hand was still limp in hers as we looked at each for a moment. Neither of us uttered a word, but we didn't have to. Her eyes were talking. And I listened to them as they spoke to me. They said, George, I hope this is okay. I'm sorry, but I couldn't hold myself back any longer . . . not with you leaving in the morning. Then I felt something else. It was my own hand. It was gradually closing on hers.

But my God, did my spirits ever take a nosedive? I had no choice but to tell myself again that it wouldn't be fair to keep leading this wonderful human being on. I damned well knew she had done everything she possibly could to make me comfortable with her—to make me want to continue our relationship and see where it might go. Only an idiot wouldn't have seen that. But what could I do? In my mind I was *dead* sure I wasn't long for this world. What had been going on inside my chest was not good. And as much as I wanted to, I couldn't stay in Deer Isle for another day; I refused to build her hopes any higher.

With our eyes still locked tight by the yearning we both felt, I was the one to break the painful silence.

"I'm sorry, Sarah, I really have to leave tomorrow. I don't want to tell you why right now. I just can't tell you. But staying any longer is not an option. Please, please understand."

"Understand?" she came back in a tone edged with a hint of anger and a lot of disbelief. "How can I understand what I don't know, George? Have you been pulling my leg all this time? Is there another . . . ."

"Hell no," I stammered, "There is no woman. Everything I told you is the God's honest truth."

Lowering my head I shook it while looking at the grass around my feet. Then I looked back at her and softened my tone again. "There's just one thing about me I *cannot* tell you. Not right now anyway. Look . . . a little time on the road will give me some time to think. I *need* that time right now. I'm sorry, Sarah. But please believe me when I tell you there is something I need to work out. I promise this isn't the end. I *will* be talking to you again. That is, if it's what you want. And if you don't . . . then, I don't know you as well as I think I do."

She didn't say anything as her eyes surveyed mine. She knew there is a direct connection not only between people's eyes and souls but their hearts as well. And she was reading mine loud and clear. A moment later, having finished her appraisal, she nodded her head slowly. "Okay, George. I believe you. I'll be waiting to hear from you."

"Fair enough," I said, "And thank you, hon. I deeply appreciate that."

With a hint of a smile rising on her face now, she asked me, "Will you at least have breakfast with me one more time before leaving? I make some wicked good biscuits and gravy, and I promise I won't put any sausage in it."

Oh no, I thought, *I've got to tell her no. She's going to think I'm a shit but I what the hell else can I do?*

Letting go of her soft hand, I took a step closer to her. I put my hands on her small shoulders, massaging them as I spoke. "I *can't*, Sarah. Maybe I'm weak but I can't go through another goodbye like this."

Immediately, my eyes began to glaze over and my heart flipped another beat, but neither meant a damn thing to me. The only thing that did matter was how lousy I felt inside for saying no again. I thought surely she was going to do an angry about-face, make a beeline to the back door of the house, go inside and slam the door behind her. But I was wrong. She didn't. And what she did next I never expected. Seeing the hurt all over my face and the mist covering my apologetic eyes her look changed. With my hand still resting on her small shoulders, she raised her own hands and put them on my hips. Then I got the shock of my life. She leaned her lovely face toward mine, just a tad, but I well knew why. She was close enough now that I could see her eyes had also gone misty. And they spoke to me. They asked me a question, four questions really. "Can I do this, George McLast? Can *you* do this? Do you mind if I do it? Can I kiss you?"

Slowly I leaned closer to her. And as I did she lifted her hands from my waist and put her arms around me. With the end of Rocky's leash still in one of my hands, I did the same thing. Feeling the rise and warmth of her breasts against my chest in the silent darkness, we only looked at each other. Neither of us uttered a word. But a moment later I did something, something I never would have dreamed I'd do. I brought my face closer to hers. Then our lips met and I closed my eyes.

It wasn't a short kiss, nor was it a long one. But it was a kiss that spoke volumes. A kiss I would never forget. And as our lips tenderly pressed together, I suddenly heard music. It was inside my head. It was old music, from the late 1960's. Playing softly, nostalgically in my mind's ears were several guitars and a single mandolin. Their sweet strums sounded as if they were coming from way off in the distance. And

they should have sounded that way, for I was listening
to the music of my youth.

Chapter 14

Before falling asleep alongside Sarah's place that last night, I had set my wristwatch alarm for 4 AM. But as it turned out I didn't really have to. Ten minutes before it was to go off the following morning, I awoke to the sound of heavy rain splattering on top of the van's metal roof. Immediately, I felt like the worst kind of creep since I planned to get up early, dress, take Rocky out for his morning business, and sneak out of there like a cowardly cat burglar. And that's exactly what I ended up doing. I couldn't help it, but I felt as if I'd made love to her during the night and was now tiptoeing out of her bedroom while she slept. Never in my life had I felt like such a cad. But that didn't stop me from playing the part. As soon as Rocky emptied out I quietly closed the back doors, double-timed it to the driver's door, hoisted him in, and cranked the engine up. No way was I going to wait and warm it up either. I just threw the transmission into gear and rolled away, ever so slowly.

Once again I couldn't help myself. This time, as I slowly approached the tree-lined road at the front of her yard, I just *had* to take a peek in my rearview mirror. With the air conditioner mounted in one of the rear windows, I could only see out of the other one. The rain was coming down so hard by now and streaking the glass that what little of the house I could see behind me in the darkness was distorted. But just as I was about to turn my eyes back to the windshield, I did see something. There was no mistaking it for anything else. A light had come on in a second floor window. I knew it had to be a bedroom window. Then I saw something else. The curtain behind it pulled to the side and there was Sarah's silhouette. I couldn't stop myself. Just as I entered that canyon of road-hugging trees, I gently tapped the horn, twice. I was saying goodbye.

But I pushed on, and as I made my way along the dark, deserted roads leading to the Deer Isle Bridge, I had all I could do not to turn that van around, stomp the pedal to the floor, and speed back to Sarah Poulin. It took all the stubbornness I could muster to keep from yanking the steering wheel and heading back. I felt the muscles in my fingers and arms tense. They wanted to spin that steering wheel as hard as they could and commandeer me back there. But they didn't. My will overpowered them as my heart set a new record of four consecutive missed beats. And each one of them fortified my belief that leaving Sarah was the right thing to do. With the windshield wipers flapping back and forth on high speed and my eyes straining to see, I howled, "No. No. No. No! You have to keep driving!" And that's what I did.

I had planned to drive all the way up to the Maine/New Brunswick border like Steinbeck had. The town of Fort Kent was there and I knew from my research it was about five hours away, even during optimum driving conditions. But as I followed the beams of my headlights through the towns of Belfast, Searsport, Frankfort, Winterport, and Hampden, all I could think about was how Sarah might be handling my leaving. And I didn't like any of the scenarios I came up with. The more miles I drove, the stronger the temptation to go back to Deer Isle nagged at me. And after I'd gotten on I-95 North in Bangor, it still hadn't stopped. With virtually no traffic on the highway; still dark out and raining hard, I said aloud, "To hell with this! I've got to get some distance between me and her, and fast. I've got to get out of Maine."

Those words had just left my mouth when I came up on the Stillwater Avenue exit. I got off 95, hung a left at the top of the ramp, crossed the overpass, and turned left into the Bangor Mall. Once in there I made another left; did a U-turn in the parking lot of a Starbucks and headed back to the highway. Despite all the state's beauty I wished I could have taken a rocket out of Maine. Other than one quick stop in Newport to gas up and grab breakfast at a Burger King, I didn't stop until I hit Massachusetts. For the entire two-hundred-mile, white-knuckles-on-the-wheel drive through horrible gray weather, all I could think about was how I was blowing a platinum chance. Over and over I ruminated about how I should have spent more time with Sarah and how happy it would have made her. And she wouldn't have been the only one. I had truly wanted to stay a while longer, too. How could I not? I was absolutely positive that she and I would have grown even closer. As it was, after spending only four days together in Deer Isle, I already felt like I'd known her for four *months.* Honestly, I can't describe how alive she made me feel. Not only that but it seemed so right when we were together that I'd finally allowed myself to believe Lorna would have given me her blessings. Because of my age I had thought for three years that I could never be interested in another woman. But I'd been wrong. I wanted to be with Sarah in the worst way now. Ever since leaving her house that morning I'd felt like an old Eskimo, floating out to sea on a chunk of ice to die alone. And again like him, since I'd turned around in Bangor, I hadn't had a clue where it was I was drifting to. That is until I exited I-495 in Massachusetts.

"Okay Rocky," I said stroking the fur on his back while steering on the ramp into Lowell, "I'm going to take you out in a minute. We're going to stop for gas again." Then I had a revelation. After remembering that Lowell was the hometown of late author Jack Kerouac, I realized I wanted to head toward Colorado, at least for starters. I decided right then and there that Rocky and I would not follow John Steinbeck's route west. Instead we'd go to the "Centennial State" the exact same way I had four decades earlier, when my buddy, Jimmy Brannigan and I had gone there to spend the summer of 1973. Thinking about Kerouac had turned a light on inside my head. Out of the cloudy-gray sky above, I remembered that the famous author and I had something in common. In his classic autobiographical novel *On the Road,* Kerouac's alter-ego Sal Paradise stayed just outside of Denver—in Aurora. And that's the same town where Jimmy and I had rented an apartment. Not only that, but our place was just off East Colfax Avenue, just as the apartment where Kerouac flopped was. That was it. The deal was done. The Rockster and I were going out there.

Since my mind was made up when I tooled down the road looking for a place to get gas, my predicament with Sarah somehow seemed a tad less troublesome. Sure, the fact that I had hurt her, and the guilt I felt for doing so, still loomed far larger in my mind than anything else. But even if only temporarily, a small dose of good news has a way of nudging our most daunting problems from the forefront of our consciousness. And as I approached a convenience store with gas pumps out front, I felt considerably better. But I didn't stop. The company that owned that store was one of two I had boycotted for years—ever since they'd fought tooth and nail not to pay for their colossal oil spills. But passing that station by was no big deal. It wasn't long before I found a Chevron station, gassed up, took Rocky out, and hit the highway again.

Eight hours later, beneath a clearing sky, we rolled into Bethel, New York. Forty-three miles southwest of Woodstock, Bethel is actually where the legendary 1969 rock concert was held, on Max Yasgur's 600-acre dairy farm. Since I had sort of been there on the night of August 15th, I wanted to see if I might be able to wake up any long-sleeping memories. I said I had "sort of been there" because I didn't quite make it to the actual festival grounds.

That wild Friday night started when a bunch of friends and I were at a discotheque in Douglaston, Long Island. It was nearing 11 o'clock when a guy we called "high-test" (because of a surely-unfounded rumor that he often got high by drinking gasoline) came stumbling into the club. He told us he had just heard on his car radio that they were no longer charging the $18.00 admission fee to get into the Woodstock Concert. His badly slurred words were difficult to make out, but we were able to decipher from his mumbling that the reason they were letting everybody in for free was because the place had been overrun by far more music lovers than were ever expected to show up.

"C'mon, let's go up there," Jimmy Brannigan said, and the rest of us didn't need coaxing.

Totally game for the adventure, I blurted, "Heck yes, let's do it! I'll go ask Rory if he wants to go. He's got the wheels."

This being back in my wilder days, with a girl I'd met earlier that night under one arm and a bottle of Rheingold beer in my free hand, I made my way through the crowded club to where Rory Harrelson was—dancing with a pillar next to the dance floor. Yes, *dancing* with the three-foot-wide, floor-to-ceiling, mirrored column. You see, our "designated driver" of sorts was tripping on LSD. It was his beat up '63 Chevy Corvair that we all had driven to the club in.

"Yo, Rory," I said, tapping him on the shoulder with my beer bottle as the band blasted out the lyrics to the Beatles' hit "Back in the U.S.S.R."

Without taking his arms off of his huge stationary dance partner, he lifted his cheek from it, swiveled his unsteady head just a bit and asked, "What's up, Georgie?"

"Guess what?" I said excitedly, "We just found out they're letting everybody into Woodstock for free. Wanna drive up there?"

"Hell yes!" he came back. "Let's do it. Just let me finish this dance and we'll go."

Minutes later, six of us piled into his burgundy Corvair and crossed our fingers so it would start. When it did we all breathed a sigh of relief and our disoriented driver cannon-balled it towards Queens and the Whitestone Bridge. Miraculously, we rolled into Bethel two hours later with everybody still in one piece. We knew we were in the right place when we saw, in the darkness, a single line of cars slowly making its way up a dirt road. On both sides of the seemingly-endless line of red taillights, were hordes of long-haired, young people in bellbottoms, hoofing it towards the festival grounds. Rather than us driving along that road though, Rory thought we'd be better off parking on the shoulder of the main road we were on. That way, if for some reason we wanted to leave before the three-day concert ended, our car wouldn't be blocked in by miles of other vehicles.

Now here I was more than four decades later, driving around the very same area shaking my head in disbelief as the memories came flashing back. And for the first time that day, I was smiling.

"Wow, we were one crazy bunch," I said to Rocky, who was standing on his seat looking through the windshield at the rural foliage all lit up by the afternoon sunshine.

We didn't stay too long in Bethel, just drove through it really. Nothing I saw seemed even remotely familiar. But that was fine. I hadn't driven far out of my way, and I did manage to recapture those memories and more. I also envisioned me and the guys walking along that road for miles. I again saw all of us crawling beneath an abandoned farm truck when the rain started pouring in the wee hours of the morning. I saw us at first light as well, when we woke up and continued up the road with the throngs of kids. I remembered seeing a gnarly-looking biker sitting on his parked motorcycle, with his "mama" perched on the seat behind him. Again I could see him take a brand new unopened bottle of Jack Daniels, slam the top of it against his bike's gas tank, and start gulping the potent contents right out of what broken glass was left on the neck. After that I saw on my mind's wide screen the ice cream truck that had worked its way up the road through that ambling sea of humanity. The driver was an opportunist—selling his cold sweet wares for three dollars a pop—literally. Lastly, how I could I forget the totally-stoned-out guy who stood tall atop a horse trailer with a beautiful blonde girl on each side of him. With hair down to his waist, almost as long as the voluptuous twins beside him, he started yelling, "Horse! I'll take three bags please!" while another man led two horses out of the trailer. He, of course, was referring to bags of heroin.

The very last recollection that entered my mind was the reason I'd always told people I was "sort of" at the Woodstock Festival. It was because before we reached the packed grounds with the huge makeshift bandstand, three of us—Jimmy, Rory, and myself were all feeling so funky from the long, wet, chaotic night, we decided to turn around. We hiked all the way back to where we'd left the Corvair and drove home.

As Rocky and I were about to leave Bethel behind, a cold empty wave of disappointment dampened my spirit. It was because I regretted that I hadn't gone the distance to the festival site. I should have done it this time around. I should have stood on the actual soil where the concert took place. After all, many people still considered Woodstock to be the definitive nexus of the counterculture generation, and I had always considered myself a part of it. But I was getting tired. And my damned heart was acting up again. With the sun shining bright through the windshield and causing me to squint, I lowered the visor and drove out of town. And as I did I began to wonder. Was it fatigue causing my heart to again skip and pound? Or was it the deeply upsetting realization that so much of my life had slipped away since 1969? Whatever the reason was, I wanted to push on and leave those bittersweet memories behind. Scranton, Pennsylvania was another hour and a half away. There was a campground just outside of it and I wanted to at least make it that far before calling it a day.

But just as Bethel was disappearing in my rearview mirror the most bizarre thing happened. I swore I heard something. It was music. And there were lyrics, too. The song sounded like it was coming from off in the distance, from behind the van. Surely, I thought, from the deserted festival site. The late Joe Cocker's gravelly voice was wafting clear as day over the treetops. He was singing his classic hit "With the Help of My Friends." And as his words continued to drift toward me, so did a mood. It was a dark mood, a funereal mood, both nostalgic and melancholic. I could feel it all around me, and it soon shrouded my soul. Joe Cocker's song had reminded me that three of the five close friends I'd gone to Woodstock with, including Jimmy Brannigan, were no longer around. And I knew that the odds were I'd soon be joining them.

But that dreary funk didn't last too long. It would soon be shaken right out of me. For right down the road more stress and distress was waiting to ambush me. And it wasn't just a memory.

Chapter 15

At about 6 o'clock, an hour after leaving Bethel, Rocky and I were closing in on Scranton. Both of us were starving and I needed to find a bathroom, fast. I exited the highway and a minute or two later steered the van into a Wendy's parking lot. Since it was dinnertime the restaurant was as busy as all get out.

"I'll be right back, buddy," I told my co-pilot, "I have to see a man about a horse. After that I'll get us some grub."

After taking care of business in the men's room, I glanced through one of the wide plate-glass windows at the van. Seeing that Rocky was okay out there, I got on one of the lines at the counter. Pleasantly surprised that my turn at the register came up so quickly, I ordered a 4-Piece Chicken Nuggets for Rocky, and for myself two Crispy Chicken Sandwiches and a small senior citizen's coffee—half decaf half high-test with two creams on the side.

In no time at all a short, stocky, middle-aged lady with a pencil lodged above her ear called out my number. Scooping the bags off the counter, I thanked her and hustled back outside.

"Okay, okay," I told Rocky when I got back into the van, "I want to take you out first." The smell of the hot food was driving him absolutely bonkers, but I managed to snap on his red retractable leash, pick him up, and put him on the asphalt outside. But just as I closed the door behind us, I noticed something. Four guys were walking our way and I did not like their looks.

Since there hadn't been any empty parking spaces alongside the building when we'd pulled into the lot, I'd backed the van into an empty spot on the opposite side of the drive-thru lane. That way I could keep an eye on Rocky while inside. At any rate, these four men, and I call them men because they appeared to be in their mid-thirties, all had their ball caps turned backwards. They had more ink on their bodies than a big city newspaper and looked as though they lived in the streets—the best case scenario might have been a dingy flophouse.

As they walked in our direction, one of the two white guys and a black guy were cursing up a blue streak—bookending every other word with a foul expletive. The short one, who I assumed was Latino, wasn't saying anything. But he had the shiftiest eyes I'd seen in some time. And ever since the scruffy crew had turned off the sidewalk and into the parking lot, he'd been shooting more glances my way than I was comfortable with. Forget the street smarts I'd acquired while growing up in Brooklyn, a frostbitten hermit from Siberia would have realized something didn't smell right. But I knew enough to keep my cool in such a situation. No way was I going to act alarmed. Instead of jumping back in the van, I stayed where I was and futzed around with the outside rearview mirror while keeping the four clowns in my periphery.

Finally, and without incident, they bopped past us and continued toward the back of the parking lot. I hadn't a clue where they might be heading but that didn't matter. I was relieved. They were that bad looking. But my relief was short lived. What I saw next drove me to a near panic. With the coast now clear, I looked down at Rocky just as I was about to lead him to the empty lot behind the van. But I didn't lead him anywhere. Instead I hollered, *"Oh God, Rocky! No, no, no!"* and yanked his head out from beneath the van. There was a bright green puddle underneath there, and his nose and mouth had been right down by it. It was antifreeze. It obviously had leaked from a car that had been parked there previously.

Instantly my body dropped like a dead weight into the squat position alongside him. Looking at the end of his snout I studied it for a split second. Then I blurted in a scared-to-death tone, "*Oh shit*, did you *drink* that crap?" I couldn't tell for sure, but I had a bad feeling he did. I must have been keeping an eye on those four losers for at least a minute or two, which was more than enough time for him to lap up a lethal dose of ethylene glycol or whatever the hell else might have been in the antifreeze.

"Oh hell, Rocky, we've got to do something! It wouldn't take much of that shit to kill you!"

Remembering that a friend once told me his dog had drank antifreeze and his vet advised him to give the dog hydrogen peroxide, I whisked Rocky up in my arms, rushed inside Wendy's, and ran straight to the head of the line where a high-school-aged girl had taken my order minutes earlier. She was talking to a customer but that didn't mean a thing. "Excuse me please, I don't mean to be rude here," I said, "but I think my dog might have just drank some antifreeze out in your parking lot. Would you get your manager please—*quick*?"

"Sure, I'll get her right away," she said. Then looking back to the man standing alongside me she added, "I'm sorry, sir. I'll be right back with you."

The older woman with the pencil behind her ear came back with the girl a moment later. After explaining to her what had happened, I asked in a desperate tone, "Would you have some hydrogen peroxide?"

The look on her face was one of concern, but she said, "I'm sorry but I don't think so."

"Okay, you must have a first aid kit or some supplies. Would you *please* take a look? There might be some peroxide. I've got to get some into this dog fast."

"Sure, let me take a quick look in back. But if I don't have any," she said, pointing down the road in the opposite direction I'd come from, "there's a Rite-Aid drugstore not a mile down that way."

After a couple of minutes, but what seemed an eternity, she came hustling back with a dark brown plastic bottle in hand. It had never been opened.

"Thank you so much. I'll bring it right back." I said over my shoulder as I darted toward the counter where they kept plastic spoons.

"No, that's okay," I heard her say, "you can keep it."

With the sun setting in the distant horizon and it getting awfully chilly, I rushed Rocky to that lot beyond the van. As soon as I stepped onto the grass, I put him down, opened his mouth, and poured one spoonful of the hydrogen peroxide way back in his throat. As I then held his mouth closed, he didn't like any of it one bit but it had to be done. And since the spoon was small, I repeated the process another time.

For ten minutes I walked Rocky in the grassy lot. The whole time he gagged and his body quaked. But again, I had no choice. I knew it was crucial that I made him vomit. And he finally did. We hadn't eaten since lunchtime, so everything he expelled was liquid—white, and foamy. For a good five minutes, he looked like a drooling rabid dog as he upchucked on uncertain legs. And the entire time my heart flipped again and again. But there was no time to worry about that. I needed to talk to a veterinarian immediately. As soon as it seemed Rocky had gotten up all that he could, I recalled seeing a sprawling discount gas station when we had gotten off the highway. I hadn't gassed up there because it had been on the opposite side of the busy thoroughfare. But it was on the right side now. Quickly I wiped Rocky's snout with a napkin, loaded him into the van, and sped up to it.

There was a payphone outside, but, of course, the phonebook just had to be missing. Although that only added to my stressful situation, I didn't hang around the booth fuming. Needing change to make a call or two, I double-timed it inside. In an urgent tone I asked the tall, thin man with slicked back hair behind the counter, "Can I have change of two dollars, please? I think my dog just drank some antifreeze. I have to call a vet, immediately."

The cashier looked at me as if I'd just climbed out of a spaceship. Seemingly not sure of what I had just asked him, he said in a slow disinterested voice, with a heavy accent I couldn't detect, "Yes. I can give you change. Will that be *all*?"

"I really don't need to buy anything right now and hate to inconvenience you," I answered him patiently, politely, "but this is an emergency. I just need the change and a telephone book, too, if you have one. There isn't one outside."

As if it was a monumental effort, he slowly nodded his head. Lackadaisically he reached beneath the counter, plunked a phone book on top it, took eight quarters out of the register, and laid them on top of the book. I could well understand why I was the only one in the store with this guy. Had I lived in that area I would never have gone back in there either. Nevertheless, I thanked him, told him I'd bring the directory back, and hurried out the door.

When I got out to the phone and opened the book, I had had a very rude awakening. It was a Sunday. It was almost dark. What vet would possibly be open for business now?

What am I going to do here? How am I going to get in to see a vet? I don't even know the name of the town I'm in! Poison Control! That's what I'll do! I'll call them!

Dog tired as I was after too many hours on the road, I certainly didn't need the negative side of my brain kicking in. But, being the screwed up George McLast I was, I just had to make the harrowing situation even worse.

My God! If something happens to him, I don't know what I'm going to do. Everything I get involved in goes all to hell. He would have been better off if I didn't pick him up in North Carolina. He'd have had a chance, anyway. A small chance maybe but a chance just the same. Dammit, I'm such loser.

With all that negativity reeling around in my head, I searched the book for Animal Poison Control. But after dialing the number and hearing the man on the other end of the phone tell me he needed a credit card number and that there would be a forty-nine-dollar charge just to advise me what to do with Rocky, I lost it.

"What? You want to charge me *Forty-nine dollars* just to tell me what I should do? You people are heartless! You have some gall! What's wrong with you? I probably have a dying animal here! Where do you get the nerve to . . . ?"

Then he interrupted me. And to my surprise the strictly-business tone in his voice changed.

"Look," he said, "the best thing you can do is to take your dog to a veterinarian. I can give you the phone number and address of the nearest one who would see you at this time on a Sunday. And there won't be a charge for that."

"Thank you, sir. Thank you very much."

Next I told him that I had no idea what town I was in. All I knew was I'd gotten off Interstate 81 and the exit number. He said it wasn't a problem and told me to hold the wire for just a moment. In no time he came back on the line and gave me the phone number and address of a vet in Wilkes-Barre—*about twenty-five miles away*. I thanked him again, called the vet, and bolted to the van. After cranking up the engine, I turned on the headlights and bee-lined it back onto I-81. And fortunately, it being the end of the weekend, traffic wasn't bad.

It was dark as we drove through Scranton. I was doing over seventy-five. Rocky had been lying in his seat next to me since we'd left the gas station. I'd been petting him, talking to him, and glancing at him the whole time. But now, as the high beams of some idiot's approaching vehicle on the other side of the median lit up my face, I saw that he had fallen asleep. And I did not like it.

"Rocky," I said, tapping his back, "Wake up, Rocky! Are you okay? Come on, don't scare me like this."

He did lift his head and look at me, but just as quickly he lowered it back onto the seat's cushion again.

"Oh no! This can't be happening!" I said under my breath, turning my eyes back to the road and gripping the wheel even tighter.

Only a second or two passed before I did something I hadn't done for quite some time. Not being an overly religious man, it wasn't often I had a dialogue with God. A *monologue* I should say.

I lit up a cigarette, cracked the window open slightly, took a hit, and whispered as I exhaled, "Please God, don't let anything happen to him. All I did was take my eyes off him for a minute or two. Please . . . if he did drink that antifreeze, let me be able to get him to this vet in time. And please let him be able to do something."

Again my damn heart was tossing and turning. My racing pulse was pounding in my temples and my ears had heated up. Everything—all my problems were becoming too, too much. I felt like jerking the steering wheel and smashing into the side of an eighteen-wheeler I was passing.

Come on, man! I thought. *Pull yourself together! As long as you're breathing you've got to handle whatever comes at you. Don't be so freaking weak. Panic and fear aren't solutions. They're short cuts to disaster. Save this dog!*

Twenty-something miles later I swung the van into the vet's driveway and only then did I realize I could have called Fred Dahlstrom instead of Poison Control when back at the gas station. The kind vet I'd met on the ferry the previous week would have told me what to do. But that was irrelevant at this point. Surely he would have advised me to take Rocky to a vet, anyway. The thing I needed to do now was get my dog into that office ASAP. And that's what I did. I picked him up and ran to the door.

When the balding, heavyset man of about fifty opened the door for us and introduced himself as Doctor Villa, he seemed to be a nice enough guy. But I didn't like the tone of his voice as I followed him into the examination room and stood Rocky on a table.

"What is this?" he asked right away as he spread the fur around Rocky's neck open with his fingertips. And turning his narrowed eyes toward mine he wanted to know, *"How* did this happen?"

I was pissed hearing that, pissed with a capital "P." And I sure didn't like the accusing look he gave me, either.

"Hold on one minute here," I said, raising my palm up and out, "I *just* found him alongside a road in North Carolina about a week and a half ago. He'd obviously broken loose after being tied up for God only knows how long."

After holding his gaze on me for a moment longer, he turned back to the healing wound. And lightening the tone of his voice once again, obviously believing what I'd told him, he said "Well, it looks like it's healing nicely. We need to check his vitals now and draw some blood.

From the opposite side of the table, I closely watched the doctor's face as he looked into Rocky's eyes and mouth. Then he felt his stomach and sides. After that he listened with his stethoscope.

"Can you tell anything yet?" I asked hopefully, as he eased a needle into one of Rocky's front legs.

"Nothing out of the ordinary," he said, as the tube of the hypodermic filled with my pal's lifeblood, "but this blood test will tell us exactly where we stand."

He slid the needle out, and as he wrapped Rocky's leg with gauze told me, "This is going to take about twenty minutes or so. You both will be more comfortable out in the waiting room. I'll be back out as soon as I get the results."

The next half hour was one of the slowest of my life. With Rocky on my lap, I tried to keep him as relaxed as possible. That was easy. All he wanted to do was sleep, which again made my mind go in directions it shouldn't have. I tried hard as I could to distract myself by looking around the waiting room.

Hanging on one wall was Doctor Villa's framed degree from Penn State. I must have read every word on it four times—signatures and all. I also looked around at the furniture I don't know how many times. Besides the sofa I was sitting on, there were two, Queen Anne wing chairs with dark mahogany legs that matched the frames of three pictures on the walls. And those prints told me something about the doctor. All three of them were of tranquil streams; two with a solitary fly fisherman casting, one with another angler fighting a fish. Of course, there was a lengthy counter along one wall, with two desk chairs behind it. Over and over I looked at all those things. And I kept looking back at Rocky as well. I stared a few times at my sneakers on the tile floor, and each time again back at him. I looked out the window at a glowing lantern on the small front lawn, and I looked back at him. The worry was killing me. Finally, the door to the examination roomed opened and the vet stepped out.

When the first thing he said was, "I have good news," my tense shoulders finally loosened up and I let out a big huge sigh of relief.

"Aw . . . that's great, doc. Thank you so much."

Allowing himself a smile as well now, he added, "There wasn't a trace of Ethylene glycol or any other toxins in his blood. You're both very, very lucky."

He walked over to us and gave Rocky a gentle scratch behind the ears. After that we exchanged a few more words and stepped over to the counter to square away the bill. He charged me considerably less than I'd expected so I thanked him one more time, paid him, and we were on our way.

After doubling back onto I-81 for a couple of exits, we finally reached that campground I wanted to stay at. By the time I checked in and drove the short distance to our assigned site, the lighted clock on the dashboard read 8:15. It had been one heck of a day, and Rocky and I both were both fall-down exhausted. Only sixteen hours had passed since we'd left Deer Isle but it felt like three days.

After snugging the van in my assigned space, between two rows of tall bushes, I took Rocky for a short walk. He needed to empty out for the night. It was pitch dark as we walked strolled through the grass and I could only see lights from two other campers. Both were a little ways off in the distance. I could hear the muted sound of a television coming from the closest one but that didn't hold my attention very long. After quickly surveying the starry sky above, I watched Rocky sniff around in the cool grass. I was so thankful to still have him with me. Years had passed since my last dog, Crispy, had died. He was a wire haired terrier that Lorna and I loved for seventeen years, and the day I buried him behind our shed we both vowed we'd never get another dog. We were that heartbroken. But as I now watched Rocky circling around, getting ready to do his business, I wondered how I had ever kept that vow. It had only been a week since I'd found him but we had become very close. Having him around seemed to add more purpose to my life. He was smart, energetic and he somehow made me feel as if my life, precarious as it was with my health issue, was far more valuable than it had been any time since losing Lorna.

After taking our walk, when we were about to climb into the back of the van to call it a night, I immediately realized something. I had left my two plastic Adirondack chairs alongside Sarah's house when I'd snuck away that morning. Again I felt like a cad for doing it. And again, as her kind lovely face reappeared in my mind, I felt like my life had more purpose. Or I should say *could have had* more purpose.

Chapter 16

After our big scare that night Rocky and I slept later than usual. And for the next two days as we headed west on I-70, just like Jimmy Brannigan and I had done so many years earlier, we took things easy. The first day we only drove seven hours, but that doesn't mean we didn't see much. As a matter of fact we witnessed one particular incident I could have surely lived without seeing.

We were beneath a gray sky just west of Pittsburgh when I decided to pull off the highway for lunch. With a red light just ahead, I slowed down as the two vehicles in front of me came to a stop. They were both pickup trucks. And the two men driving them, who looked to be in their mid-thirties, jumped out. Immediately, they rushed towards each other, got in one another's faces and started yelling. My windows were closed so I couldn't hear what they were saying, but by the time I came to a full stop, the one who'd been driving the truck in front of me reared back and slammed his fist square into the other guy's face. That I did hear. I had just rolled my window down, and the "thud" was sickening. It sounded like a baseball bat smashing a cantaloupe. The man on the receiving end of the punch was about the same height as the other guy but much, much thinner—skinny as a rail in fact. I thought for sure he'd go down like right now. But he didn't. What happened next was one of the strangest chains of events I'd ever seen.

Although the guy with the buzz cut hair who'd delivered the punch was built like an NFL linebacker, the tall, scraggly one wiped his hand beneath his nose, took one quick look at the blood, and started swinging to beat the band. And I mean *swinging*. His fists were flashing back and forth so fast they were nothing but a blur. And as if being hit by two super-charged, high-speed pistons, the big guy's head kept jerking back so hard I thought for sure his neck would crack. He was now defenseless. All he could do was cover his face, or try to.

With all the lunatics on the roads in this day and age, I was apprehensive to get out of the van. But feeling like I had to do something, I reached for my door handle as the bodybuilder went down to his knees. Then it got really weird. The thin guy immediately stopped swinging, and he actually helped the other guy to his feet. With an arm around his waist he then walked him back to his truck. Once he got him inside he said a few words to him, got back into his truck, and took off through the green light. A moment or two later the pickup in front of me finally pulled away as well, albeit not nearly as quickly.

As I proceeded down the four-lane road, looking for a place to get a bite to eat, I took something away from what I had witnessed. It wasn't that the fight in the dog can sometimes be more important than the dog in the fight. I already knew that. I'd seen a similar scene take place in a Bedford Stuyvesant schoolyard when in high school. A tall, skinny friend had fought one of the school's star football players and pounded him down to the asphalt. What I took away this time was different though. When I first saw the two men get out of their trucks and start fighting, I thought, what is wrong with this world? Why can't all men simply talk out their differences and feuding countries do the same? Granted, in my younger days, I, too, had been in some godawful knock-down, dragged-out fights. But at least I learned. After all, we are the supposed most intelligent of all animals. We have the ability to think deeply; to reason. Like scientists who build on the knowledge left by the scientists before them, why can't human behavior evolve into something better? However, what I just took away from what I'd seen was not all negative. It was a lesson in hope. And it allowed yet another ray of sunshine to break through the dark, seemingly-impenetrable layer of clouds I previously believed shrouded all of mankind. Despite the greed-driven agendas of so many world leaders and the macho-at-all-costs attitudes of so many men, the winner of the fisticuffs I had just seen actually helped his attacker get up from his knees. Disheveled as he was he may not have looked like much, but he had done what was right. And it was obvious he cared about his fellow man.

As I drove further west on I-70 that unseasonably-warm autumn afternoon, Sarah Poulin was again first and foremost on my mind. The more miles I put between her and me, the more I missed being with her. Time and again when passing exits I felt like getting off the highway, crossing the overpass before me, and flooring it all the way back to Deer Isle, Maine. But I couldn't. I couldn't chance having her fall for me harder than she already had. As much as I wanted to drive up her driveway again and lean on the horn as I approached the house, I couldn't bring myself to going back there. Not yet anyway. Not unless I saw a doctor and somehow, by a long shot, had gotten a clean bill of health. No, when something is seriously wrong with a person, they usually know it. And I was by now positive that whatever was going on inside my chest and occurring more and more frequently was terminal. That was the one and only reason I kept driving west.

The remainder of that afternoon was uneventful for the most part. Other than stopping once for gas, Rocky and I stayed on I-70 the entire time. The only interesting thing I encountered was another memory from my Denver trip with Jimmy. Staring out the windshield, my eyes seemingly glued in a hypnotic trance on the mundane road before me, I remembered how the two of us saw something we never had before. Back in '73 there had been white shapes painted on the road every so often—shapes of human bodies. We thought the first one we saw was an awfully strange thing to see on a highway. But after driving my beat up Plymouth over a few more we figured they'd been painted there to mark the scenes of fatal accidents. That and to instill safety in the minds of all passing motorists. And it surely worked. Every time we saw one it captured our attention, albeit in an eerie, morbid way.

A few hours after that memory passed, my little buddy and I called it a day. With at least another hour of daylight left, we pulled into a real spiffy campground outside of Canton, Ohio. After slowly motoring through the entrance and past a pond surrounded by trees, I saw the office up ahead and beyond it a bit of the grounds. All around me the grass was manicured like a putting green on an exclusive golf course. Everything was impeccably maintained, and I began to understand why the site fees had been so high when I'd checked my campground directory earlier. Some of the trees surrounding that pond were adorned with extravagant bird houses. Beneath their limbs fancy, inviting, evenly-spaced benches had been placed as well, though nobody was sitting on them. Both sides of the paved entry road were lined with a long row of cedar flower pots—brimming with healthy, vibrant pansies of every color imaginable.

Up ahead, beyond the office, were a few recreational vehicles set up for the night. But they were all huge. Every one of them was the size of a rock star's private bus and every bit as extravagant. Instead of a campground, I felt like I was pulling into one of those upscale, gated communities they had back in Florida. Don't get me wrong, I was by no means a slob. But still, the orderliness of this place made me uncomfortable. I would have preferred a down-to-earth place to spend the night, with a dirt road and natural surroundings. But it was what it was. Since I was ready to relax and kick back for a while, I was not about to turn around and go hunting for a more comfortable place to stay. So I parked in front of an office that looked like a miniature Swiss chalet, got out of the van, and walked inside.

"Hello," I said to the short man behind the counter who, with his wide suspenders, put me to mind of something else Swiss—a yodeler, "I'd like a site for one night, please."

Right away he gave me the once over with chipmunk-like eyes that seemed too large for his face. And just as quickly, he tilted his head to the side like a nervous ferret and peeked out through the office's front window. Knowing exactly what he was doing, I didn't like it one bit. Neither did my heart. It again started doing the rumba.

"Ah," he finally said, dragging the sound out while thinking what he would say next, "I'm afraid we don't normally allow vehicles that are not specifically designed for camping."

Now I disliked him even more. But when I had checked my directory earlier I'd seen there were no other campgrounds in the area. And as I mentioned before I did not want to have to go hunting for another place to stay. There was no way that, without a fight, I was about to go back to the interstate and drive who knows how much farther.

"Listen," I said in a calm tone as I placed my palms on the counter and leaned slightly forward, "it's the end of the season. I can see you don't have many campers out there. All I want is a place to sleep tonight. I don't care if you put me in an isolated site at the far end of the campground."

I could tell I had struck a chord. He took another glance outside at the van but after that he looked down at a map beneath the plate glass on his countertop.

Without raising his eyes he slowly nodded his head saying, "Hmmm, one night you say?"

I knew it was a stipulation. He wanted to be reassured that I'd have my old van the hell out of there the next day. And since I'd be handing over forty-five dollars, plus tax, it in no way deepened my love for him. But he was holding all the cards. Sarah had been on my mind all day and I just wanted to park the van beneath a tree somewhere and be left alone.

"Okay, I can put you over here in site 47," he said with his head still down, pointing on the map to a far corner of the campground with his tiny finger.

"Sure, that would be fine," I came back when he looked back up at me. But as I filled out the registration form and squared away the fee, I said as little as possible. I bit the bullet, went through the motions, and was damn glad when I walked out of there.

The site turned out to be extremely nice. I was all alone at the fringe of the campground where it bordered a forest. What made it even nicer was that there was an oak tree next to the site, and its thick limbs formed a canopy no more than three feet above the van's roof. But that got me thinking. I realized right away that none of those big fancy rigs could have

157

possibly fit beneath all the limbs and branches. And that knowledge made me dislike the yodeler even more.

"To hell with him," I said to myself after killing the engine, "I'm going to enjoy the privacy here all the same."

Once I got situated and had taken Rocky for a walk, I pulled out the propane stove and heated us up some chicken hotdogs, sauerkraut and a can of low-salt green beans. By the time we finished eating the sun had dipped below the horizon. With no Adirondack chairs to sit on, I stayed where I was on the picnic table bench and fired up an after-dinner smoke. And just as I did I saw something moving in the dusky light. It was the little man with the Napoleon attitude. He was driving a white golf cart, coming in my direction. And with no other campers anywhere near me, I knew he was about to pay me a visit.

Oh hell! I can just imagine what this clown is going to say when he sees me smoking. I am not going to take any holier-than-thou nonsense. Obviously, he has more than his share of hang-ups. Why couldn't he have just left me alone here?

Sure as hell, he steered the cart directly into my site. Rocky started to bark and I thought that was all I needed. Now he'd have another nonsensical reason to give me the boot.

"Shush, Rocky," I said leaning forward, rubbing his back as our unwelcome visitor stopped the cart and got out, "it's okay."

"Evening," he said, eyeballing the cigarette in my hand as he walked toward me.

"How are you doing?" I came back in a strictly-business tone while giving him what I felt was a mandatory nod.

Coming to a stop maybe six feet away, he reached into his pants pocket, pulled out a small metal box and extracted a cigarette. Talk about being surprised. But that was nothing. What he was about to tell me would really shock the pants off me.

"I hope you don't mind me stopping by like this. I just wanted to tell you something."

As he paused to light his cigarette then, I said, "No. It's no problem." But I was still apprehensive.

Exhaling smoke, he said in a surprisingly apologetic tone, "Look, I didn't mean to come across so rudely back at the office. It's just that I bought this place six years ago and it was a shambles. My wife and I have done an awful lot of work upgrading it and, well . . . as you can see we cater to an upscale crowd. Anyway, I, ah, I just wanted to apologize for coming across like such a hard ass."

I could not believe it but I was now actually starting to like the guy.

"Hey, don't worry about it," I waved him off, "I suppose, from a business point of view, I can understand why you have to be careful."

He shifted his eyes to the end of the bench I was sitting on, pointed to it, and asked, "Do you mind if I have a seat? It's been another long day."

"No. Sit down. I certainly know what long days are all about."

As soon as I said that a frisky squirrel leaped down from a tree trunk near the front of the site. It took one tentative hop in our direction, spotted Rocky lying at my feet, and quickly bolted across the road.

"My name's Pete," the small man said, extending his hand, "Pete Svenson."

I shook it saying, "Nice to meet you, Pete. As you probably saw on the registration form I filled out, I'm George McLast."

159

"Where you heading to?"

"Right now Colorado. After that I'm not really sure."

"Must be nice to go be able to go wherever you want," he said as if he'd been trapped for a long time.

I leaned over, rubbed the ash of my finished cigarette into the dirt and laid the filter on the wooden table. "Yeah, it is nice. I'm taking my trip on a shoestring, but it's something I want to do before I . . . well, while I can."

With a look of genuine concern beginning to appear on his face then, he said, "Oh?" as if it were a question.

Looking away from him, I turned my eyes to the squirrel still hopping in the grass across the road. "Yeah," I said, "I . . . I've got a bit of a health issue. Don't know the severity of it yet, but I know I've got a problem."

There was a short break in our conversation. I knew he was wondering whether or not he should ask what my problem was, but he didn't. He was an intelligent man. He knew that prying might be crossing a line. Instead he said something about himself. And it made me like him even more.

Turning his head toward the road now, but seemingly looking beyond it at nothing in particular, he said, "Yeah. I've got problems myself. I have MS. My muscles lock up on me sometimes. As a matter of fact, just last week I was getting out of my pickup and they did it again. I fell to the ground. And my wife had to help me up."

"Oh, that's a shame," I said sympathetically, thinking he couldn't be past his mid-forties yet, "I'm really sorry to hear that."

"Yeah," he said, his eyes now scanning the campground but surely still not seeing much of it, "I was perfectly fine when the misses and I bought this place six years ago. At that time I could work from sunup to dark. And I did, seven days a week for four years. The place was in really sad shape because the previous owner had let it go all to hell. And his clientele, well, let's just say they were one rough-around-the-edges crowd."

"It's obvious you put a lot of work into it. This is by far the cleanest, most meticulously-maintained campground I've seen since hitting the road."

"Thank you. Brenda and I bought it for a really good price. We'd sold my auto repair business and slapped the entire proceeds down on it. Our plan was to turn it into what it is today, hold onto it for about twenty years, and flip it for a handsome profit. Now we realize that's not going to happen. I can't keep the pace up. Shit . . . in four or five years I probably won't even be around."

At this point my heart really went out to him. No, I couldn't stand the sight of him when we'd first met an hour earlier. But now it was different. Now I felt like I was talking to a friend, and truly feeling sorry for him. But then again, if any of my beliefs had been reinforced since setting out on the trip, it was that human nature can be impulsive and unpredictable. Yes, sixty minutes earlier I felt like leaning over the counter in this man's office and slapping him across the face, but now I wanted to encourage him.

"Look, Pete, all you, I, or anybody else can do is what we're capable of. That's it. We must do the best we can with what we have to work with. And that holds true whether we're talking about money, education, or . . . or whatever time we might have left on this planet."

As soon as those optimistic words left my mouth, they stunned me. Ever since my heart had done its first summersault months earlier, I had been thinking like a doomed, apocalyptic pessimist. But now I, of all people, had given myself hope. After all, who could say for sure that I was all that close to the finish line? How the hell did I know my condition was definitely terminal? Maybe, just maybe, I actually had five, ten, even twenty years left. Maybe I could lick this thing, whatever was causing it.

After saying goodbye to Pete Svenson ten minutes later and wishing him well, I was still full of renewed hope. That deep, all-knowing voice that sometimes speaks inside my head was still repeating a sentence I had told Pete. *We must do the best we can with what we have to work with. We must do the best we can with what we have to work with.*

Off and on for the rest of the evening, I kept hearing those words. And later on, as I lay in bed in back of the van, I heard them one last time. And when I did they brought on my second revelation of the day.

Go back to her, I thought, *you don't need to rekindle old memories in Denver or anyplace else. You're not dead yet. Go back to Sarah and make new memories. You know she cares for you deeply. You know your relationship with her would only grow stronger. You even know deep inside that Lorna would rather you be happy than keep on living the life of a miserable hermit. Forget your heart problem. You can tell Sarah about that and have a doctor check the damn thing out afterwards. For crying out loud, go back and spend some time with her. You know something would become of it. Crank this old van up first thing tomorrow morning and beeline it back to Deer Isle.*

Chapter 17

Just before dawn the next morning I headed back east on I-70. Following the swath my headlights cut into the darkness, I drove faster than I had when driving west. With the highway all but deserted and Rocky back to sleep alongside me, I wondered whether or not I should call Sarah later on. But I didn't think about it very long. I didn't debate with my reasoning. I wanted to surprise her. I still wanted to pull into her long driveway, make my way through the trees, and hit the horn once her stone house came into view. I planned to time the two-day ride so that I'd get there after dinnertime. That way I would be fairly certain she'd be done working for the day and more than likely at home. With my mind made up and spirits high, I reached toward the console for the coffee I'd bought at a Waffle House restaurant. But just as I wrapped my fingers around the foam cup something happened.

"Oh my God," I said as my face suddenly tightened up, "what is this?"

My heart had skipped again. But this time there was more than just pressure accompanying it. Now it hurt. The pain didn't last more than a split second, but it radiated from my chest all the way down my arm— my left arm. Had it continued it would have been paralyzing. I wouldn't have been able steer the van. But still I wasn't out of the woods.

Although the pain had quickly subsided, I now felt as if red-hot water had been injected in my veins. And it seemed like the sides of the van and the windshield were closing in on me.

"Oh, no," I cried out, "I don't need this! Please. Please God, not now!"

I was having a problem breathing, too. I did manage to suck in a breath, but I barely managed to draw in enough air. It was like trying to inhale with both sinuses blocked up.

It's probably just your nerves, I tried to convince myself, *you've had a lot going on. You haven't been exercising since leaving Florida. That always calms you down, no matter what might be bothering you. On top of that you've been driving all over creation. Driving is tiresome, and you're not a kid anymore.*

Coming upon an exit by now I saw some lighted signs up ahead.

Alright, that's better. You're breathing easier. Now look over there. It's another small town with all the usual signs. Focus your mind on them. Okay, there's a McDonald's, a Fairfield Inn, a Ramada, a Cracker Barrel, a Burger King and Arthur Treacher's.

By the time the glow of all those businesses were behind me, I was feeling somewhat normal again—still shaken up for sure, but at the same time relieved.

As the day wore on and more miles piled on the odometer, I kept trying to assure myself that what happened had been a freak occurrence. But it still bothered me. And for the rest of the day my heart continued to miss beats more often than it ever had before.

At sunset that evening, Rocky and I pulled into a campground outside of Poughkeepsie, New York. And, as always, the first thing I did was hook up the water and electric. But this time there would be no sitting outside the van. It was that cold—cold enough that I had to turn the portable heater on as soon as it got dark. Not wanting to sit behind the wheel and read, I decided to take a brisk walk. Still convinced that I hadn't been exercising enough, and feeling guilty about it, I pulled my watch cap on my head and snapped Rocky's leash on his harness.

As we started to hoof it around the circular road that made a wide sweep through the campground, I saw that again we almost had the place to ourselves. By the time we finished our first lap, I'd only seen four RVs. Their owners had all been inside them because of the cold and that was fine by me. The last thing I needed was to have to act sociable. All I wanted was to get my heart rate elevated and keep it that way for a while. Plus, I had things on my mind.

As cold mist streamed from both my nostrils with every quickening breath, I started in on myself. I began to wonder if that revelation I had before falling asleep the night before in Dayton was really a good idea. I began to doubt that doubling back to see Sarah was the right thing to do.

I don't know, I thought as I passed one of the RV's with its lights on inside, *should I really be going back there? Yeah . . . I can explain to her what's wrong with me right away. But what if my problem does turn out to be serious? Will she wish I hadn't come back? Will she wish she'd never seen me again?*

As I continued around that circle beneath a starry sky, I stressed big-time. I entertained the idea of packing it in—heading back to Florida the next morning. And the instant that option crossed my mind the faulty muscle inside my chest stalled again. This time it set a new record. It missed four beats in succession. Was it a message? Was it a warning that I'd better get my tail home to see Adam, my daughter-in-law, and granddaughter before the lights went out permanently?

Hoping that picking up the pace might help me forget what I'd just felt in my chest, I jogged faster. I also hoped it would nix any temptation to go back to the state I detested. And it worked, temporarily at least. My heart's rhythm smoothed out. And not long after that Sarah Poulin's beautiful image again graced the forefront of my mind. Sure, I loved what little family I had left, but I was not going to panic and run back to Florida. I wanted to spend more time with Sarah. I wanted to give *us* a chance.

But as Rocky and I passed by the van and started our last lap, my worst enemy started in on me. I wished there was a switch I could throw to turn off my mind every time it bombarded me with unwelcome thoughts. But there wasn't. And again I had no choice but to listen to that know-it-all basso voice inside my head. It told me there was a strong possibility Sarah was now glad I had left. And that she very well could be thinking we had rushed things when we'd been together those few days. Then the damned voice insisted that even if she did want to see me—even if she had been glancing out her bedroom window with hopes of seeing me come up the driveway, it still wouldn't be fair to her. After all, who was to say that after going back to her I wouldn't find out I had a chronic disease or even die on her.

Tired of listening to it all, I finally snapped in a gruff tone, "Freak this crap!" And I said it loud enough that Rocky looked up at me with a concerned look.

"It's okay," I said to him, "I didn't mean to upset you. Let's pick up the pace, Buddy."

And we did. With me leading him like a mechanical rabbit does racing greyhounds, I jogged faster than I had in years. Partly because I wanted my heart to implode if it was going to, and partly because I hoped to sidetrack that negative train of thought. I didn't want to believe that Sarah might not feel the same way about me as she did when I left Deer Isle.

If all an aging man has left is fear and uncertainty, there's no sense in him going on. That's what I told myself and that's what I believed. "Let the son of a bitch blow up," I whispered under my quickening, heaving breath now, "I'm going back to Maine no matter what kind of crap my subconscious throws at me. That's it. My mind's made up. There are times when a person needs to gain control of their thoughts. And this is one of them. If she backs off after I tell her what's wrong with me, so be it. That'll be another thing. But I *am* going to see her."

That night, as I slept sound as a newborn baby, I dreamed about Lorna. Although I rarely remembered my dreams, I did this one. It began when we were young—when we had gone on a date to the Long Island Game Farm out in Manorville, not far from The Hamptons. There was a monkey in a cage, and when I said hello to it, its face took on a perturbed look. "Okay, the heck with it," I'd said, jutting my face closer to the cage, trying to be cute in front of Lorna, "you obviously got up on the wrong side of bed this morning." But mister monkey didn't like my attitude. No sooner had my last words left my mouth when the disgruntled primate spat at me. He'd caught me off guard for sure, but I did manage to jerk my head far enough to the side to get out of the line of fire. Looking at Lorna then, my eyes wide agape with amazement, we both went hysterical.

That had really happened, and so had all the rest of my dream. It was as if I was watching a succession of video clips—snippets of many happy experiences Lorna and I had shared together. But there was something really odd about the dream. Although I hadn't thought about most of the events in it for years, they all seemed as though they'd never been far from the forefront of my mind.

You would have thought that, after dreaming about all those carefree times with Lorna, I would have been heartbroken when I awoke in the back of the van the next morning. After all, they were gone and so was she. But I had mourned for those three years and had by now begun to accept my loss. And as dawn's first light brightened the blue curtains surrounding me, lying there on the mattress with my eyes resting on the headliner up above but not really seeing it, I knew it was alright to move on with my life. Nothing, but nothing, was going to keep me from going back to that stone house in Down East Maine. Come hell or high water I was going to see Sarah by the end of the day. And when I did I would lay my uncertain cards on her table.

Chapter 18

Knowing that Deer Isle was an eight-hour drive from Poughkeepsie, I took my time before leaving the Hudson View Campground. Though I hadn't seen much of the place the evening before, when I stopped into the office for a cup of the free coffee, the low-key, but nice enough, seventyish lady at the desk told me there was a trail that led to the Hudson.

"Really," I said, "is it a long walk?"

"No, not at all. It's about ten minutes. And is it pretty! We're only about a week from peak foliage season. Your really should see it."

Glancing at the wall clock behind her, seeing it was only 8:15, I said, "I'm easy. You talked me into it."

"You might bring a camera if you have one. It's that pretty."

Although I didn't have a camera, I thanked her for letting me know about the trail, then Rocky and I headed toward it. The morning air was crisp and clear, and I was glad I'd worn my hooded sweatshirt. There was virtually no wind, but the temperature couldn't have been any higher than forty. The narrow, well-worn trail cut through a strand of lofty oaks and elms—all of them bursting with color. It was one of those mornings when no matter what might be ailing you, you were awfully glad to be alive.

After trekking about three-quarters of the way to the river, I suddenly stopped Rocky, saying, "Hold on, pal. Do you see what I see? That's something else."

Just before the trail made a sharp turn to the right, maybe fifty feet in front of us, a squirrel and baby rabbit were almost nose to nose studying each other. Then the damnedest thing happened. The bunny darted around the tree trunk they were next to, came right back, and again stared at the squirrel. Not to be outdone, the gray squirrel did the exact same thing. It hopped over to the trunk, stopped for a second or two, and turned its head back to the bunny as if to say, "Oh yeah! Watch this! I can do the same thing!" Then, in a flash, the squirrel ran around the wide trunk, came back, and stood square in front of its new friend again. I couldn't believe they were playing such a game. But as Rocky and I watched they did it two more times. They might have kept at it but after that we started walking towards them and the squirrel spotted us. It dashed into the woods with the young rabbit not far behind.

As Rocky and I continued along the trail, I wondered why on earth human beings couldn't be as friendly as the animals I'd just seen. Why do so many people feel it's necessary to put on facades? Why do so many seem to think only of themselves? Why has it gotten to the point where we expect people to be so aloof? Yes, that was what I asked myself. But I didn't dwell on it very long because as soon as we reached that crook in the trail where the rabbit and squirrel had been, there was the Hudson River in all its autumn glory. Adorned on both sides by unspoiled forests bursting with color, it was a breathtaking view with gold, orange, and different shades of red everywhere—a sight that would give hope to the staunchest of pessimists.

As planned we knocked around until 10 o'clock before hitting the road. And for the rest of the day my optimistic mood didn't desert me. Passing through Danbury, Waterbury, and Hartford on I-84, and that maddening strip of 395 through Massachusetts, I knew I was doing the right thing. As far as I was concerned there was no doubt that north was the direction I needed to be heading. And when I once again crossed the bridge from New Hampshire and touched down in Maine, the same relaxed feeling I'd felt the last time ran through every fiber in my body. The state felt so right to me, and so did returning to Sarah Poulin.

My upbeat mood lasted for the next four hours. But in the darkness, just after 6 PM, while rolling down that same hill toward the lights of the Deer Isle Bridge my troubling doubts returned.

"Well Rockster, this is it." I said, glancing at him beside me, giving him a couple of pats. Then I picked up my pack of cigarettes from the console. "I've got just about enough time for a quick smoke."

There are times in our lives when we know things we must do are not going to be easy. If we are somewhat distant from them, whether that distance is measured in time or in miles, it tends to make them seem less difficult. But as we close in on those trying tasks, our perception of them often seems to change. And mine was changing fast. I now dreaded telling Sarah about my malfunctioning heart far more than any other time that day. But I tried to fight off that dread.

Come on, man! You are a man, right? What you're doing here is the right thing. It's got to be done. Just toughen up, bite the bullet, and do it.

Minutes later, I spotted the Poulin Lane street sign in the beams of my headlights. I was closing in on the moment of truth. Feeling as if I was listening to a tension-building drum roll, the pit of my stomach tightened. But I pushed on. I turned right at the sign, mashed my smoke out in the ashtray, and narrowed my eyes. Would she be home yet? Part of me hoped the answer was yes. I wanted to get this over with. The other part of me hoped her Subaru wouldn't be in the driveway. That way I'd have more time to rehearse what I had to say. But none of that mattered. After a

171

slight jog in the road I saw the house, and her SUV was parked alongside it.

The part of the lawn closest to the house glowed from the light escaping the first floor windows. It was so quiet that even with the van's windows closed I could hear the gravel crunching beneath my wheels. Although I couldn't hear them, it felt like a frenzied swarm of butterflies had been released inside my knotted gut. And the closer I rolled to the house the faster those wings seemed to beat.

Okay Georgie, this is it! There's no backing out now.

Then I saw her. Just as I had the early morning I'd left, I could only see her silhouette. But this time it was gone as quickly as it had appeared. And seemingly as fast as a fireman slides down a firehouse pole the front door opened. And there was Sarah.

To hell with all the rest, I thought, *I'm glad I came back.*

By the time I slowed to a stop she was standing alongside the driveway waiting for me. Looking through the window on Rocky's side, at her standing there with her arms crossed in the cold, she was a sight for sore eyes. She was smiling. It was a wide smile and it spoke to me. It said, I am so, so glad to see you George McLast. And when I got out and walked around the front of the van towards her, she said the exact same thing, minus one "so."

"I am so damn glad to see you George."

Uncrossing her arms, she held them out. And when I came up to her she threw them around me.

"I'm really glad to see you, too, Sarah," I said, taking her in my arms and holding her warm body close to mine. No longer were there any doubts. This was where I belonged. This woman and I were meant for each other. I knew I had done the right thing. I also knew that the goose bumps I felt rising beneath the sleeves of my sweater had nothing to do with the cold.

Entwined the way we were in each other's arms, she leaned her head back and her cheek left mine. And still holding each other as if within our grips were the most precious things on God's green earth, we looked in each other's eyes. Without uttering a word, with the front light of the house reflecting in her eyes, they asked me if it was alright to kiss me. Then she saw the answer in mine. They told her hell yes. Ours lips slowly drew closer to each other's and they met. But then something ruined that kiss—that moment—that wonderful reunion.

My entire body suddenly quaked. I let out a moan, no, a grunt. I let go of Sarah and grabbed my left arm. Instantly, she knew something was very wrong.

"What is it, George? My God! What's the matter?"

It was the same paralyzing pain I'd felt a day earlier after leaving the campground in Dayton, Ohio. But this time it wasn't just a jolt. This time it wasn't subsiding.

Gripping my arm, doubled over in the darkness now with the back of my head to Sarah, I gasped as I said, "I, I don't know. It's got to be my heart. I've been having some strange feelings in it for a while now."

"Oh, Jesus," she said, trying to keep her fear out of her voice but failing. "Wait right here. I'll go get my car keys. I'm taking you to the hospital right now."

"No, wait! Hold on!" I came back, using all the strength I could muster to straighten myself up. Then I jammed my hand into a front pocket of my jeans and pulled out my keys. "Don't leave, please. Here, take these. We'll just take my van, Rocky's in it and we'll get there faster that way."

"No! We can't take him to the hospital, George," she came back, snatching the keys from me, "I'll take him into the house quick. He'll be fine with Lewis and Clark. Can you get in the van?"

"Yeah, go ahead. And hurry," I croaked, handing her the leash.

There was no need to tell her to hurry. She swept Rocky up into her arms, ran to the door, put him down just inside the threshold, and slammed the door closed. By the time she came bolting back, I'd climbed into Rocky's seat but hadn't even closed the door yet.

"Here, I'll get that!" she ordered, giving it a shove closed and then running around to the driver's side of the van.

"Which key is it?" she asked, holding them toward me as soon as she jumped in behind the wheel, "two of these look like car keys."

"This one," I moaned, tapping the right key with a fingertip.

She gave me a quick but gentle squeeze on the back of my neck, slid the key into the ignition, and turned it. During the split second it took for the engine to turn over, she shot one quick glance at me before throwing the tranny into reverse. I had never before seen such deep concern on anybody's face.

"I'll be okay," I said, after she peeled the van backwards and rammed the gearshift into drive.

"I'll have you at the new hospital in less than fifteen minutes. Had I called an ambulance, it could have taken it ten just to get here."

"Whatever you think is best." Then I added, "If I should lose consciousness or, or worse, would you call my son Adam in Florida? His number is in my wallet."

"Of course, I would. But you're going to be okay, hon. Is the pain getting any worse?"

"It's about the same," I said, realizing that my palms were sweating profusely as I let my head fall back on the seat's headrest.

174

But somehow hearing Sarah call me "hon" seemed to lessen the pain. And as she steered the van off of Poulin Lane and onto the paved road, something else dawned on me. I knew that if I lived through the jam I was in, my having a screwed up heart wouldn't mean a thing to her. She would still care for me. She would still love me. And knowing all that, despite my chest, shoulder and arm still feeling like they were in a vice, I felt the grimace on my face ease a little.

As Sarah tore through the dark countryside, I rolled my head on the headrest and looked over at her. With the lighted dashboard casting a faint green glow on her face, I saw it was riddled with determination, deep concern, and unadulterated fear.

"Sarah," I struggled to say in a weak voice, "maybe you ought to slow down. If there're any cops out here they'll stop us for sure."

"Good!" she came back. "They can escort us the rest of the way to the hospital."

Glancing at me then, she reached over the console and put her hand on my shoulder. "Don't worry. I'm going to see to it that you come out of this just fine."

Her words were consoling even though we both knew that besides getting me to a doctor as fast as she possibly could, she really wouldn't have any say about the outcome of my grave situation.

As we both turned our eyes back toward the road, a car came around a bend up ahead and approached us with its high beams on. When the driver quickly lowered them, I said, "I want you to know that I'm awfully sorry about this."

"*Sorry?* What on earth are you talking about *sorry?*"

"Well," I strained to speak again, "my heart has been acting up for a few months now. It's been missing beats from time to time, and every time it kicks back in it *really* kicks. It feels like it's bouncing off my rib cage. And I mean hard. But when we met, and for the four days we spent together after that, I . . . I just couldn't bring myself to tell you about it."

"Oh," she came back, dragging the word out before following it with, "so that's why you didn't stay longer, isn't it?"

"Yeah," I admitted, "I wanted to stay. I really did. But I felt like you and I were . . . well, connecting. You know, we were . . . ."

"Yes, I know," she interrupted as she steered around that bend in the road. "But let me see here. What you're trying to tell me is that you didn't want to get too involved, because you had this thing going on?"

"Yes, that's it in a nutshell." I said, looking at her face again. "I didn't think it would be fair to you. And to be honest I was afraid it might, well, turn you off."

With worry still all over her angelic face, she managed to smile. It was a small smile, an ironic smile, but a smile just the same. Then, giving me a disbelieving glance, she looked back over the steering wheel and said as if what I had said was the most ridiculous thing she'd heard in years. "So you thought it would turn me off, did ya? Well let me tell you something, bub. This Down East country girl hasn't felt the way I do about you for a long, long time. Believe me when I say I never would have dreamed I'd invite a man I just met to stay at my place. I only invited you because . . . ."

She didn't get to finish what she was saying. She didn't have the time to because I suddenly let out a long, loud, frightful "Awww!" then said, "I'm sorry, Sarah, but it's this pain. Oh shit! It's killing me now! It feels like a Sumo wrestler is jumping up and down on my chest! The pain is crushing!"

The SUV lurched ahead even faster now. She'd floored the gas pedal. The force of the vehicle accelerating shoved me so far back in my seat I thought the backrest was going to give and I'd wind up in the seat behind me. And right then, as if in an instant all my blood had been sucked out me, my entire body went slack. Slouched motionlessly in my seat, everything started spinning—the floorboard beneath my feet, the entire van, my body and my mind.

"Godammit George!" Sarah shrieked. "You hold on, do you hear me? We're almost at the hospital! Please, for God's sake hold on!"

Maybe a minute later she slammed the brakes and we skidded to a stop. She yanked the gearshift into park, killed the engine, and blurted in the most despairing voice I'd ever heard, "I'll be right back! You're going to be okay! Stay with me dammit!"

That said, she bounded out of the van and tore toward the emergency room doors like a madwoman. Totally helpless, it took all the strength I had to turn my head and watch her through the window. And the second she disappeared inside that was it. The lights on my mind's screen went dim. I was still consciousness, but barely. And by the time they wheeled me through those doors on a gurney, all I could hear was what sounded like distant voices—that and the whoosh of my failing pulse ever so slowly pushing through my temples and neck. I thought for sure that each labored breath I took was going to be my last. Then I heard nothing. All I can recall after that is lying flat on my back with my paralyzed eyes watching white ceiling tiles rush by as they hurried me down a hallway. That's the last thing I remember before blacking out. And when I say I blacked out, I mean blacked out, totally. There was no bright white light at the end of some tunnel. My life didn't flash before my eyes either. My mind simply shut down completely. And although I had no way of knowing, things got even worse.

The doctors and nurses worked on me frantically but my damaged heart had a mind of its own. It had had it. It stopped cold. The monitor they had rigged me up to flat lined. The painfully slow, dying succession of beeps they'd heard stopped. It was replaced by the steady high-pitched tone of hopelessness—that cold electronic announcement of death. I was gone. There still was no bright white light and there wouldn't be.

Hurriedly they hooked up a defibrillator and turned it on. Once, twice, three times, my lifeless body jerked but my heart did not respond. They did it a fourth and fifth time, too, but again to no avail. But Doctor Franklin J. Fillmore III made one last attempt. The electrical charge again jolted through my body, and this time it worked. After being clinically dead for one minute and twelve seconds, the charge restarted my heart.

As I said, I, of course, don't remember any of it. But all the details were explained to me after I'd been stabilized. What was also explained to me was that I had blockage in one of my coronary arteries, and I would be taken by ambulance to Eastern Maine Medical Center in Bangor to undergo open heart surgery.

Yes, I was alive. And that was far better than the only other dismal alternative. But when Doctor Fillmore left the room with me being weaker than I ever imagined any living person could possibly be, and knowing I was still in one hell of a bind, I felt as good as dead. But that dreadful, soul-crushing feeling didn't last long. For a short time later the door just beyond the foot of my bed opened, and I saw Sarah again. She looked so, so worn, yet she was still as beautiful as ever. And she was smiling.

With her eyes fixed on mine she walked to my bed and sat on the chair beside it. Then lowering her face she eased her warm soft cheek next to mine. Gently she put her arm around me as if it was the most natural thing in the world, as if she'd done it a thousand times before, and she whispered in my ear, "I told you you'd be alright, George. And I'm going to make sure you stay that way, for a long, long time."

I was sure then, that despite needing the open heart surgery, I would be alright. I also knew I'd be spending the rest of my life with Sarah Poulin. And it turned out I was right on both counts. What I didn't know, though, was that after I bounced back Sarah would be so insistent that I lived out my dream. Not needing a whole lot of convincing, she and I went out and bought a used, but super nice, RV. And this coming May the two of us along with Rocky, Lewis, and Clark are going to hit the road. We're going to take the cross-country trip that I'd never completed.

Also by Tom Winton

Beyond Nostalgia
The Last American Martyr
Four Days with Hemingway's Ghost
Within a Man's Heart
A Second Chance in Paradise
Forever Three
The Voice of Willie Morgan and Two Other Short Stories

52891267R10099

Made in the USA
Charleston, SC
02 March 2016